Capital Bride

CYNTHIA WOOLF

ISBN: 193888714X
ISBN-13: 978-1938887147

DEDICATION

For Jim. My husband, my lover, my best friend, my rock.

CONTENTS

ACKNOWLEDGMENTS

Many thanks to my critique group, Michele Callahan, CJ Snyder, Karen Docter, Jennifer Zane and Kally Jo Surbeck.

Thanks also to my editor Kally Jo Surbeck.

CHAPTER 1

New York City   April 10, 1867

On the other side of the door was her last resort. Either this or prostitution and prostitution was not a choice. She couldn't raise MaryAnn in that environment, nor if truth be told, could she lower herself to live like that. At least this way there would be some stability in her little girl's life.

Sarah took a deep breath, turned the knob, and walked through the door to a better future for her daughter and, if she were lucky, for herself.

The office was small and precisely kept. A single desk with a straight, high backed wooden chair, one in front and one behind, sat in the middle of the room. She'd noticed the flowered curtains were open on the way in, tied to the side. The small area was flooded with dazzling afternoon light. The walls were whitewashed and the desk well organized. There were several tables with neat piles of files along one wall. The other wall held several rows of pictures of women and men. None smiling, as that was the way pictures were taken, but all appeared to be wedding pictures. Below each picture was a small brass plate with the names of the bride and groom and the date of the wedding.

A small, woman in her late thirties with fiery red hair, sat behind the desk. When Sarah got closer she saw gorgeous dark blue eyes behind the wire rimmed glasses perched on the end of her nose. Her eyes were so dark a blue they could almost be called violet. They were striking and clear, honesty shone from them along with a "no nonsense" attitude.

"May I help you?" the woman asked.

"Um. Yes. My name is Sarah Johnson. I saw your advertisement for mail order brides."

The woman looked Sarah over, taking in her clothes, her hands clasped in front of her and ending at her face.

"First, let me introduce myself. I'm Margaret Selby and I own Matchmaker & Company. Please, sit down. You're older than the women we usually have. You're also better dressed and don't appear to be hungry. What would bring someone like you to my door?"

"I've been living with my great aunt. She passed away suddenly two weeks ago and the lawyer says I need to find other lodgings. My cousin, William, has inherited everything except a small stipend she left for me. William is selling everything. MaryAnn and I have nowhere else to go."

"MaryAnn?"

"My daughter."

"So, you are a widow?"

Now was not the time to be less than truthful, if she wanted this woman's help. "No."

"I see. How old are you, Miss Johnson?"

"I'm twenty-eight."

"And your daughter?"

"MaryAnn is five."

"Tell me, Miss Johnson, how did you come to find yourself with child at age twenty-two without being married? Surely you knew how those things happened by that age."

"My fiancé was killed at Bull Run."

"I understand. Many fine men were killed there and throughout the war."

"Yes, there were. Lee and I planned on marrying before he left. He still had two weeks before he was supposed to go back. He was sure the war wouldn't last long," she sniffled and blew her nose into her handkerchief. "They called him back early, and then he was killed."

"No need to go into further detail,

Miss Johnson. Let's get down to business, shall we?"

Sarah sat straight in the chair. "Yes, of course."

She was more nervous now than she had been showing up on Aunt Gertrude's doorstep six years ago, pregnant and unwed. They'd planned on putting out the story that Lee was her husband but one of the servants overheard and passed the information on to other servants, some of them in the homes of her Aunt's friends.

Aunt Gertrude took it all in stride. She actually handled it far better than Sarah had. She'd cried for days until Gertrude shook her and said to get under control and stop feeling sorry for herself. So she'd had her beautiful MaryAnn and was raising her with Aunt Gertrude's help. She would be missed for so many reasons.

"Miss Johnson? Miss Johnson." Margaret snapped her fingers bringing Sarah back from her memories.

"Yes, Miss Selby. I'm sorry."

"It's Mrs. Selby. Now, please pay attention. I have several candidates that might work for you. Two farmers in Kansas and a rancher in the Colorado Territory."

"Do you have a recommendation?"

"Well, neither farmer has children, though they are not unwilling to consider a woman with children. It would be awfully lonely for your MaryAnn with only you and her new stepfather for company. The rancher, on the other hand, also has a daughter, who is seven, I believe. They would be able to keep each other occupied while you attend to the work you'll need to do. Can you cook?"

"Yes. Our cook taught me the basics. If I have a recipe, I can follow it."

"Then, I suggest you write down all of your cook's recipes. You'll need them no matter which man you choose."

"I've already got the ones I want. I'd hoped to put them together in a book one day. These men you're talking about, how old are they?"

"Raymond Jacobsen, a farmer in Kansas, is thirty-two. Robert Kline, also a farmer in Kansas, is twenty-nine, and last is John Atwood, a cattle rancher in the Colorado Territory. He's a widower, thirty-seven and has a daughter who is seven. I think he would be the best match for you."

"Have you checked out these men?"

"Of course. I'm very thorough, Miss

Johnson. I have an associate who travels for me and talks at length to each of our bachelors. We don't have any brutes or other disreputable types with this agency. You can put your mind at rest."

"Thank you. What do I do now?"

"I'll need the name of your aunt's lawyer to confirm your story, your current address and references, if you have them. Your cousin would probably be one to list. Neighbors who have come to know you would also be good ones. You see, we check out our ladies just as thoroughly as our gentlemen. I'm staking my reputation on you, Miss Johnson. I don't intend to see it tarnished. That said, I understand that given your circumstances, there might not be a lot of people willing to give you a good reference. Rest assured that I take that into consideration."

Sarah nodded. "I understand completely. Can you help me?"

Margaret Selby had seen her share of desperate young women. Those who were hooked on laudanum or its brother, opium. They didn't make it. Sarah, with her manner and good clothing, was a lady through and through. But was she good material for a frontier wife?

Margaret got up, went around the desk and scrutinized the young woman in front of her. She cut a fine figure. Pretty blonde hair and sky blue eyes. Serviceable wool coat. A short high-necked, long-sleeved jacket that hit her at the waist. It matched her skirt perfectly, obviously made from the same bolt of cloth. Expensive. Well made. She would work well for Mr.

John Atwood and his daughter, Katy. No need to tell Sarah that Katy wouldn't talk and hadn't since she'd witnessed her mother's murder two years ago. No, Sarah, MaryAnn, John and Katy would all do well for each other. Margaret was sure about that and, so far, her record was unblemished.

"In answer to your question, yes, I believe that we can be of benefit to each other. My assistant will be around to talk to you this afternoon. Please make sure you are available."

"Of course. I'm going to collect my daughter from our neighbor and then plan on being home after that."

"Very good. I'll contact you tomorrow morning with my decision but I feel, based on our interview today, that it will be a favorable one."

"Thank you, Mrs. Selby. Thank you very much."

The young woman left, and Margaret was alone with her thoughts.

A few hours later, her man returned with his report.

She had one of the two former Pinkerton detectives she employed check Sarah's story and references. All was as she claimed. The report stated that she'd been living with her great Aunt Gertrude who had died, suddenly from a heart attack two weeks ago. Her fiancé was dead, died at the battle of Bull Run July 21, 1861. Daughter, MaryAnn, born April 11, 1862. Everything checked out. She would arrange for Sarah and MaryAnn's passage on the train to Denver.

She sent a note to Sarah.

April 10, 1867

Dear Miss Johnson,

I believe we will be able to aid you. Return to my office on 7 May. I will have your train tickets available. You will be going to the Colorado Territory to wed Mr. John Atwood. The train leaves on the 8 May and arrives in Denver on the 15 May.

Sincerely,

Margaret Selby, Proprietress, Matchmaker & Co.

As soon as she was finished with her letter to Sarah, she began writing her letter to John Atwood.

11 April 1867

Dear Mr. Atwood,

I believe I've found the perfect bride for you. Her name is Sarah Johnson. She is twenty-eight years old and has a five-year-old daughter named MaryAnn, who I believe will be a great friend to Katy. Both of your daughters will benefit from this alliance.

Please pick up Miss Johnson and her daughter at the train station in Denver on Wednesday, 15 May.

Sincerely,

Margaret Selby, Proprietress,

Matchmaker & Co

She dusted the letter to dry the ink, then carefully folded it and placed it in the envelope she'd just addressed. It would go out with tomorrow's mail, and reach Mr. Atwood within ten days, she hoped. That would give him plenty of time to prepare for Sarah and MaryAnn's arrival.

Margaret smiled to herself. This would be a very good match. She felt it all the way to her bones.

*****

Sarah got off the trolley four blocks from home. At least, it had been her home for the last six years. She'd always known that she and MaryAnn lived here by Aunt Gertrude's good graces. But she hadn't expected her to die, at least not so soon.

Gertrude had been her great-aunt, that was true, but she was her paternal grandmother's youngest sibling and was only two years older than Sarah's own father, who severed all ties. He'd thrown her out when she'd gotten pregnant. Aunt Gertrude had been her salvation.

She walked up the steps to the door of the three story brownstone. There was no one to open the door for her any longer. William let all the servants go, with good references and the small stipend that Aunt Gertrude left for each of them.

William was really being very decent about it all. He'd kept the servants on for more than ten days after Gertrude's death and he'd put off selling the house as long as possible but now it was listed and would probably sell in no time. Sarah couldn't dilly-dally any more. She had to put her grief aside and "get on with it" as Gertrude would say.

Sarah entered the foyer and untied her bonnet, hanging it on the peg above the hall side table where she normally placed the mail.

"I'm in the sitting room, Sarah," called William.

She walked through the door and over to where he stood by the fireplace to kiss his cheek. "William, how are you? I hadn't expected you until Sunday."

"I'm here with some news."

Sarah's stomach clenched. "News?"

"Yes, I might as well get right to it. I've sold the house. You and MaryAnn will need to be out by the end of the month."

Stricken, Sarah said, "William, we

have nowhere to go until the 8th of May."

"If it were socially acceptable I'd have you come live with me, but..."

"You'd never find a wife with a tainted woman and her bastard child living under your roof."

"Sarah—"

"No, I'm well aware what society thinks of me. They've been very open in sharing it."

William took a deep breath. "So, I've arranged for you to stay at the Booking's Boarding House until you find other lodgings, which it sounds like you have. What are you going to do?"

"I'm getting married."

"Married?" He turned his back on her and faced the fire warming his hands. "I hadn't realized you were engaged."

“I’m becoming a mail order bride. It’s the only way I can start my life over. I can’t stay here.”

He turned back to her and took her hands in his. “You could always stay and marry me. At least, you know me.”

“You’re my cousin and though it may be legal, you know that I find the thought repellant. Not that I don’t love you but not in the way you want.” She took her hands from his. “I just can’t. You’ve been more than kind to me and if….”

“No. Don’t worry. My generosity is not dependent on you becoming my wife. It will not change the arrangements I’ve made for you.”

Sarah let out the breath she hadn’t realized she’d been holding. “Thank you. I have to go next door and get MaryAnn.

Mrs. Adams has been kind enough to watch her for me while I've been looking for work."

"I take it nothing has panned out so you are taking this drastic step?"

"I've only been a mother. I'm not qualified to do anything else that would support us."

"Very well. I shall leave you to it." He picked up his hat and gloves from the side table next to the sitting room door. "I will see you on Sunday, as usual. You can fill me in on your plans and this man you've promised to marry."

"You know," said Sarah, "you really should consider proposing to Caroline Kendall. She does admire you very much."

He stopped, cocked his head just a bit and asked, "Does she now? Do you think she'd accept my suit?"

"I don't know why not."

"Well, you don't seem to have any problem turning me down." He stepped closer, eyes dropping to her lips for a brief moment. "Sure you won't change your mind?"

She stepped back with a fond but regretful smile. "I'm sure."

"Then perhaps I should call upon Miss Kendall. I do need to consider a wife and heir to continue the Grayson name."

"Yes, you should."

"Goodnight, Sarah. Until Sunday."

"Sunday. Perhaps you would like to bring Miss Kendall with you to luncheon?"

"What a splendid idea! You can act as chaperone."

"I'll prepare something special."

"It's a good thing that Cook taught you what she did. I must admit you do a fine job."

"Thank you."

"Well, goodnight then."

Sarah followed him out and went next door to get MaryAnn. She always tried to let her daughter stay with Mrs. Adams as long as possible. It did them both good. MaryAnn struggled to understand Aunt Gertrude's death and Agnes Adams missed her grandchildren who had recently moved to Boston when her son's law firm sent him there.

She knocked on the door.

The butler opened it. "Ah, there you are, Miss Johnson. Please come in. You'll find Miss MaryAnn and the mistress are having tea in the parlor. May I take your hat and coat?"

Sarah smiled and handed her things to him. "I don't know how you do it, Peters. How can you keep up with those two fireballs? I'm surprised you're not having tea with them."

"I was invited, Miss, but had to decline. I had other duties to attend to."

They walked together to the parlor. Peters opened the door and held it for her. What she saw made her smile. Agnes had had Peters bring down the small table and chairs from the nursery. She and MaryAnn were at the tiny table drinking tea and eating strawberry scones with clotted cream. One of MaryAnn's favorites, as Agnes knew perfectly well.

MaryAnn looked up when Sarah entered the room.

"Mama," she said in a very stately tone, "we're having High Tea. Mrs. Adams says this is what they did when she was a little girl."

Sarah smiled. She enjoyed watching her daughter with the old woman. "How nice of her to share this with you." She turned to Agnes. "I hope she hasn't been much trouble for you."

"Not at all, my dear. I enjoy having her here."

"I'm afraid it's only for another couple of weeks. William has sold the house and MaryAnn and I will be leaving the city on May eighth."

"Sit down, dear, and have a cup of tea. Then tell me all your news."

Sarah took one of the small chairs at the little table.

“Tea?” asked Agnes.

“Yes, please.”

“MaryAnn, would you please pour a cup for your mother?”

“I’d be delighted,” answered her little girl, so grown up. Sarah’s heart twisted in her chest. MaryAnn had missed so much being raised without other children. She was so mature for her five years.

“Now, my darling. Tell me where you’ll be headed.”

“I’m hoping we’ll be leaving for the Colorado Territory. A place called Golden City. It’s the territorial capital, so not too small a city, I hope. Perhaps once we are settled and it looks to work, you’ll come out.”

Mrs. Adams nodded. “And what will you do there?”

"I'm getting married."

"Married!"

"Yes. You might as well know. I signed on to be a mail order bride. The gentleman I'm going to marry is a cattle rancher and has a daughter around MaryAnn's age. It'll be good for MaryAnn to have a playmate."

"That's awfully far away. Couldn't you marry someone closer?"

"Agnes, you know that's not possible. The only one who would have me is cousin William and I find that idea totally unacceptable. He is my cousin, after all."

"Understandable. But that doesn't change my wish you could find someone right here in New York. I'll never understand society's shunning of you. You shouldn't have to pay for one mistake for the rest of your life."

Though she didn't see her beautiful daughter, conceived in love, as mistake, she simply smiled. "Thank you but you know the only way I could stay here is to marry William or turn to something unsavory. I'm not qualified for anything else."

"What about a governess?"

"No one wants a woman who has been 'soiled' anywhere near their children for fear that my lack of morals will somehow rub off on them." She took a sip of her tea.

"Mommy, what is 'soiled'? Doesn't that mean dirty?"

"Yes, sweetheart, it does."

"How can you be dirty? You wash all the time."

"Yes, I do, don't I?" laughed Sarah.

MaryAnn nodded vigorously. “And you make me do it, too.”

“Anyway, I will write you,” said Sarah, hoping to distract MaryAnn.

“Mommy.”

“Yes, dear?”

“How can you be dirty and clean at the same time?”

I’ve wondered the same thing myself, thought Sarah, but she said, “Time to tell you the truth. Some people think that because I wasn’t married when I had you that I’m soiled.”

“But you said that Daddy died before you could get married. So it’s not your fault.”

“Most grownups wouldn’t agree with you, sweetie. They think your daddy and I were wrong to share our love before we were properly wed."

"But aren't we supposed to share our love with other people?"

"Yes, we are. There are just some rules about grownup love that you don't understand yet."

MaryAnn slowly shook her head. "I think it must be real hard to be a grownup."

Surprised by her baby's insight, she asked, "Why do you think so?"

"'Cause. You got to 'member a whole bunch of kid rules and then there's a whole bunch of grownup rules and you got to 'member all them, too."

Sarah chuckled. "I think you have the right of it. What say you, Agnes?"

The old lady wore a smile. "I'd say you are correct, Miss MaryAnn. And it doesn't get any easier the older you get because there's a whole other set of rules for us old people."

"Agnes, would you care to join us for Sunday luncheon? William will be coming with Ms. Kendall and it will be sort of a farewell celebration."

"That would be lovely. Remind Peters on your way out, would you?"

"Of course. Say goodbye, MaryAnn."

MaryAnn went to Agnes and gave her a hug. "Goodbye, Mrs. Adams. Thank you for having a tea party with me."

"You're quite welcome, dear girl. Quite welcome, indeed." Agnes hugged her back like she'd never let her go. It was going to be especially hard to say goodbye to her. Agnes had been Sarah's rock since Aunt Gertrude died.

Sarah took MaryAnn's hand and they

walked down the stairs where Peters waited with their coats and hats.

"Thank you, Peters. Please remind Mrs. Adams that she is having Sunday luncheon with us. It will be served at one o'clock."

"Yes, Miss. I shall endeavor to remind her and will escort her myself."

"Wonderful, you shall join us as well."

"Oh no, Miss. It's not done. I shall return here and wait until it's time to come back and retrieve my mistress."

Sarah nodded. "Very well. We'll see you on Sunday."

As they walked home MaryAnn asked, "Where is Colorado Territory?"

"It's west of here a very long way. It's going to take us many days to travel there. Do you think you can be an especially good girl for Mama while we travel?"

"Yes, ma'am. I heard you say he has a little girl. Will she be my sister if you marry her daddy?"

"Yes, I guess she will. Do you think you'll like having a sister?"

She thought about it a minute before answering. "I think I will. It'll be nice to have someone small to talk to."

Sarah smiled. "Yes, it will, won't it?"

They reached the house and went inside. The fire William built was burning low. Sarah added more wood.

In front of the fireplace were two wing chairs. MaryAnn sat in one of them. She looked so small. Her eyes, the pale blue of Sarah's own, sat in stark contrast to the inky black hair and eyelashes she'd inherited from her father. Except for the eyes, MaryAnn was a miniature of Lee. Everyday Sarah was reminded of the man she loved, whose face would be faded from memory if not for her daughter. MaryAnn kept him alive. Even so, his strong jaw and boisterous laugh were all but gone.

In manner, MaryAnn was totally unlike her father. He'd been fun loving, teasing and always joyful. She was solemn and thoughtful. So much like her mother.

"Mama, why are you crying?"

She hadn't realized tears trickled from her eyes. Sarah sat in the other chair. "I was just thinking about your father. Come here and let me hold you."

The little girl dutifully got up and went to her mother, sitting on her lap and relaxing in her arms.

"He was a good man, your father. Don't ever let anyone tell you differently."

"I won't. How old was he when he died?"

"He was twenty-two, just like me. We'd been sweethearts for as long as I can remember and always knew we'd get married, but then the war started and he went off to fight. I didn't see him for so long. He came home wounded. Shot in the shoulder, and we decided to get married as soon as he got out of the hospital. The date was set for the following Sunday. He was called back on Friday. With only a few hours together before he left again, we made the most of them. We made you."

"Why does it make you sad when you look at me?"

"Oh, my darling, I'm not sad when I look at you. I'm so happy to have you and love you so much. I sometimes cry because I know your daddy will never get to know you."

"Will I have to call this new man, Daddy?"

"No, not if you don't want to." She squeezed her daughter. "Now enough serious talk. Let's go to the kitchen and make luncheon. I'll even make us some hot chocolate. What do you think about that?"

Sarah saw her eyes sparkle before she scooted off Sarah's lap. "I'd like that very much please."

"Good. Let's see what we have to eat with that."

Sarah watched her little girl skip to the kitchen, their serious talk forgotten with the prospect of a sweet treat.

CHAPTER 2

Sarah hoped some day to publish a book of recipes. That's why she'd written down all of Cook's recipes. But it wasn't just to make a book, which she still planned to do, but because she needed them, to use them. She had them carefully tucked away in one of the four steamer trunks she brought. Each trunk was filled to bursting with clothes, shoes and books. She may be going to the frontier but she that didn't mean she couldn't be civilized.

Before they left for the boarding house she'd gotten out her grandmother's wedding ring. She'd never worn it before because everyone knew she wasn't married. Now though, they didn't know and it would stop a lot of questions she'd rather not answer. The plain gold band fit perfectly on her finger. She felt her grandmother's strength with it on, that she could face anything. When she married Mr. Atwood she would wear his ring on her left hand and her grandmothers on her right.

Sarah and MaryAnn arrived in Denver on May 15th at half past four in the afternoon. They'd spent seven generally uncomfortable days on several different railroads to get there. MaryAnn had been a blessing, making friends with other people on the train along the way. Even so, Sarah didn't care if she never saw another train again. She was tired and cranky, definitely not a good traveler, unlike her daughter, who seemed more excited with each new landscape they crossed.

Sarah'd had enough prairie, corn fields and cattle by the second day out of Chicago. Denver sat at the foot of the Rocky Mountains. Magnificent in their grandeur and a blessing to Sarah because it meant their trip was at an end. She was to meet Mr. Atwood here at the station.

The porters unloaded her trunks and she had MaryAnn stand beside them, while she panicked. One of the trunks was missing. Until she unpacked them she wouldn't know which one.

"What do you mean one of my trunks is missing? How can you mislay a steamer trunk?"

"I'm sorry Ma'am. We'll find it and send it to you when we do." The poor conductor was almost as upset as Sarah.

She took a deep breath and tried to calm down. "Very well. Here is the address of where I'll be. Please send the trunk there as soon as possible."

He accepted her ticket and handed her a receipt back. "Yes, Ma'am. Again please accept my apologies."

She nodded and walked back to where MaryAnn stood.

It was May, but the chill air gave Sarah shivers. She pulled MaryAnn closer to keep her warm. MaryAnn taking a chill was the last thing that Sarah needed. The trunks blocked part of the wind that whistled by the open platform, but none of the cold.

In a short while, a large man pulled up driving a long wagon with side boards. He had dark coffee brown hair that brushed the collar of his black wool coat and was graying at the temples. With his vivid green eyes he was one of the handsomest men she'd encountered in some time. Why would this man need a mail order bride?

Next to him was a little girl with hair as pale as MaryAnn's was dark. She had the same green eyes as her father. The black coat she was growing out of revealed the hem to her light blue dress peeking out the bottom. This had to be Mr. Atwood and Katy.

He jumped down and then held his arms up to the child. The girl fell into them and wrapped her arms around his neck. There she buried her face, clearly not wanting to meet her new stepmother and sister.

He carried her up the stairs of the platform stopping in front of Sarah. Now that he was closer she saw that his green eyes were rimmed with dark lashes and stood in sharp contrast to his dark hair. Sun, wind and laughter had left lines at his mouth and eyes, giving him character. His face was very pleasing with a sexy shadow of stubble on his strong jaw.

"Mrs. Johnson?" His smooth baritone washed over her, leaving her with a little tingle of awareness. One she hadn't felt in years. Not since before Lee died.

Sarah nodded. "Yes. Mr. Atwood?"

"Yes. This is Katy," he smiled down at the girl in his arms.

"Hello, Katy. I'm Sarah and this is

my daughter MaryAnn," Sarah said. She placed her arm around MaryAnn's shoulders pulling her into her side.

"Hello," said MaryAnn.

Katy turned and looked at MaryAnn, then buried her face in her father's neck once again.

"Katy doesn't speak."

"Oh. I'm so sorry," said Sarah.

"Don't be. It's not that she can't talk, she just doesn't. I'll explain later. I've made arrangements to stay at the Melvin Hotel for tonight. It's one of the finest in town. Then if you're still willing, we'll get married by the Justice of the Peace here in Denver tomorrow and head back to Golden City right after."

"I believe that will be splendid." Her heart raced a bit and she found she was nervous and excited at the prospect of becoming this man's wife. "As you can see we came to stay," she waved at the three trunks. "I'm glad you brought a big wagon, although we are missing one trunk. The railroad seems to have lost it during one of the train changes we went through to get here."

"I'm sure they'll find it. I just hope it wasn't something you'll need right away. Did you give them our address?"

"Yes, I did." Sarah's stomach took that moment to decide to grumble with hunger. She placed delicate hands over her fine flat stomach drawing attention right to where she'd rather not have, knowing she was flaming red with embarrassment, "Oh, excuse me."

"Good. By the way, the wagon is

called a buckboard. I wasn't sure how much baggage you'd have. Let me get those loaded up and then," he smiled hearing her stomach grumble, "we'll go get some supper."

An hour later they were seated in the hotel dining room. Sarah ordered roast beef with mashed potatoes and gravy for herself and MaryAnn. Mr. Atwood got a steak, rare, with fried potatoes on the side and fried chicken with mashed potatoes for Katy. All of the food looked wonderful. Sarah realized just how hungry she was for a real meal.

MaryAnn enlivened the conversation and Sarah was grateful for her ability to put adults at ease. "What kind of ranch do you have Mr. Atwood? Do you have horses? Can you teach me to ride? We used to see riders at the park in New York."

He put down his fork and knife, wiped his mouth with a cloth napkin and gave his full attention to MaryAnn. Then he smiled and it transformed his face, making him seem friendlier, less stern.

"Well now, Miss MaryAnn, I raise cattle, but we do have horses that would be gentle enough for you and your mother." He glanced over at Sarah, his green eyes warm and friendly. She shook her head no. "Or not. You don't have to learn to ride."

Sarah felt herself flush under his gaze. "So, tell me about yourself, Mr. Atwood. Why would you need a mail order bride? This town looks plenty big enough for you to have found a girl to marry."

"That's just the point. I don't want a girl. I want a woman. One who might be able to help Katy. And to be completely honest, I don't have the time or inclination to court a woman"

Katy's eyes narrowed and her murderous gaze went to her father. Clearly she didn't like being the topic of conversation.

"I'll do my best."

"I'm sure you will. Mrs. Selby thought Katy and MaryAnn would do well together."

Sarah nodded. "I hope so. This is delicious." The flavor burst on her tongue and made her mouth water. "I'd love to ask the chef for the recipe. We haven't had a real meal since we left New York."

"What did you do for food?" Concern rode his features.

"At some of the stations there were

housewives selling boxed lunches and I brought apples, cheese and bread with us in my valise. We had a seven day picnic."

"I'm sorry the trip was so long." There was a modicum of guilt that showed in his eyes.

"Don't be." Sarah felt herself blush again. "MaryAnn quite enjoyed herself. She's a much better traveler than I am."

MaryAnn echoed the sentiment. "Mama got tired of the scenery not changing. Not me. I just kept looking for new things. And they were everywhere. Saw lots of animals. A man on the train told me the huge things were antelope and they were good eatin'."

Mr. Atwood laughed again. The deep baritone sound reached deep into Sarah. Her body reacted in a way she hadn't felt in years. People's heads turned and the women's eyes lingered on his very appealing face. "Well, your friend's right about that. I used to hunt them. That was before we got the cattle operation going and antelope, deer or elk were what we ate."

As supper ended and she'd finished a wonderful piece of apple pie, Sarah tried to stifle a yawn. Seven days sitting up on a train was definitely beginning to wear on her. "Oh, pardon me. I'm afraid we need to retire for the evening. It has been a long trip and I think it's catching up to me."

Mr. Atwood rose from the table as Sarah stood. "Completely understandable. Shall we meet here in the morning at say," he pulled a pocket watch from his pants pocket, "six am?"

"Oh. So early? What time do you

have set for the marriage ceremony?"

"Nine."

"Oh my, well what if we make it seven then? In the spirit of compromise, of course. We do want enough time to have breakfast beforehand."

"That's agreeable." He nodded his head and a lock of hair fell forward. It was all Sarah could do not to reach over and gently put it back in place. She itched to run her fingers through his thick, brown locks.

Sarah noticed that both girls were almost silent during the meal. It might be normal for Katy but it most certainly was not for MaryAnn.

"You've been awfully quiet this evening, sweetheart," she said to her daughter.

MaryAnn looked over at Katy.

"Maybe she don't have nothin' to say. Maybe that's why she don't talk."

Katy looked up at her father for help.

He nodded to her and then said, "Katy doesn't talk because she witnessed her mother's death. I'll explain later."

"John, may I call you John?"

He nodded his head. Tension weighed on his shoulders. The change in his countenance told her he felt guilt about his wife's death and perhaps Katy's muteness.

"You and Katy need to know, I'm not trying to replace your wife or her mother. We want to find our own place in this family, not usurp your wife's."

"Dorothy. Her name was Dorothy." He said it softly, almost reverently.

"I'm not trying to take Dorothy's place." If she hadn't been across the table from him she'd have taken his hand in hers. As it was, she hoped her face conveyed her sorrow at his loss. It was all she could do for now.

"I understand that and so will Katy if she doesn't now." He looked down at his daughter, squeezed her hand and got a watery smile in return. "We'll all be fine, you'll see."

She took MaryAnn's hand and they walked to their room on the second floor. John and Katy were next door so they walked up together.

"MaryAnn, you go into the room. I'd like to talk to Mr. Atwood."

He nodded at Katy, "You too. I'll be right there."

"You wished to discuss something, Sarah?"

"You were going to tell me why Katy doesn't speak."

He nodded, closed his eyes for a moment and took a deep breath. "She witnessed her mother's murder during a bank robbery. Katy was the only survivor and she hasn't spoken a word since."

Sarah put her hand over her mouth. "Oh my gosh. I'm so sorry. When did your wife…die?"

"It's alright. You can say it. Murdered. She was murdered in cold blood two years ago." His eyes clouded over and his voice softened. "She was seven months pregnant."

"How horrible for Katy to witness."

He ran his fingers through his hair. "The doctor's say she'll talk when she's ready. The sheriff wants her to talk now.

She's the only witness and they still haven't caught the people who did it."

"Thank you for telling me. I'll do my best to help her."

"I know you will. Goodnight, Sarah."

"Well, goodnight then." She put her hand out for a shake.

He took her hand in both of his. "Goodnight, Sarah." His big hands enveloped hers with heat and strength, a rare sense of comfort. His rough calloused hand was so different from her much smaller, soft one. Yet it felt wonderful. She wondered what those rough hands would feel like against the smooth curves of her body.

Sarah looked up to see his brown eyes piercing her with what could be called passion or like herself, with loneliness. She retrieved her hand and bowed her head.

"Goodnight John."

She went into her room where MaryAnn waited sitting on the bed.

"Mama, why are you red in the face?"

"I'm just a little flushed. I got hot in the dining room, that's all."

"Oh, okay. I thought maybe Mr. Atwood done somethin' to you when he shook your hand before and maybe he did it again. That's when you got red."

Sarah felt herself flush again at the memory.

"You must be hot again, huh?"

"Yes, sweetheart. I'm hot again." She waved her hand in front of her face knowing it wouldn't do any good. It wasn't that kind of heat.

*****

They arrived at the dining room in the

morning at seven sharp. John and Katy were already seated. John had a cup of coffee and Katy a glass of milk.

He stood as they approached. He was dressed in a black suit with crisp white shirt and string tie. He held a black hat that looked new.

“Good morning, Sarah and Miss MaryAnn. You both look lovely today.”

“Good morning John,” she looked over at Katy. “And you too Katy.”

MaryAnn went and sat next to Katy then turned her attention to John. “Good morning, Mr. Atwood. You’re going to be my father now and Katy will be my sister. Isn’t that right, Katy?”

Katy nodded.

“I think I’m going to like having a big sister. Mama says you’re seven. That’s older than me. I'm five. Mama says I'm too grown up for my age."

Katy nodded and grabbed MaryAnn's hand. Sarah thought it was a wonderful show of acceptance on Katy's part. MaryAnn held her hand and chattered all through breakfast which was just as well. Sarah was nervous. Her hands were sweaty and shook a little. She was glad to have the coffee cup to hold on to. Her stomach was full of butterflies and she could barely eat. After all, it wasn't everyday a girl got married.

"You both look very nice this morning. Even a new hat for the occasion," said Sarah.

"It's a Stetson and I thought I'd try and make an impression. Did it work?"

She laughed, some of the tension

easing. "Yes, you've made a very good one."

"So do you." His eyes raked over her. Sarah wore a dark peacock blue wool suit that accentuated her eyes. The fitted jacket emphasized her small waist and gave her an hourglass shape other women would have died for and all without a corset. "It appears we are all in our Sunday best."

Even the girls wore their best clothes. She'd dressed MaryAnn in her red velvet dress with black collar and matching coat. Katy had on a pretty pink dress with ruffles at the bottom and dark pink ribbon at the waist. She, too, had a matching coat.

John picked up the buckboard from the stable. He'd paid the stable owner to watch over the trunks so he wouldn't have to unload and reload them. He helped her and the girls onto the wagon. She and John sat on the bench seat, the girls in the back with the trunks.

It was a short trip from the hotel to the Justice of the Peace's office. Only about a five minute walk but John wanted to leave right after the ceremony so they took the buckboard.

Even at this early hour the streets were crowded with pedestrians, wagons, buggy's and horses with riders. So much so that it took them fifteen minutes to navigate through the heavy traffic to the courthouse.

John's ranch was about twenty miles west of Denver and it would take more than four hours to get there. That's why he wanted to leave right away.

They would arrive home in time for her to fix dinner…no it was supper out here in the west. She'd have to remember that. Dinner was luncheon and supper was dinner. Whatever it was called they would get to the ranch about two o'clock and she would have enough time to unpack MaryAnn's trunk and then fix it.

They got to the Justice of the Peace's office and suddenly it was all real. All other thoughts flew right out of her head, replaced by butterflies in her stomach. It must have showed on her face.

His hand enveloped hers with that same warmth and strength she'd felt last night. Only she felt something else today, confidence. "It's going to be alright, Sarah."

She took a deep breath. "I know. I know it will."

"We're going to be a family now, right Mama?"

Sarah realized with MaryAnn's question that she might not be the only one who was nervous about today. She smiled at her precocious daughter. "Yes, we are and together we can do anything."

She looked up into John's smiling face, noticed the way the dimples creased his cheeks and still couldn't believe her luck. He was so handsome and about to become her husband.

John helped them all down and they walked into the building. Once inside they found the office. A very thin, gray haired woman sat at a desk outside the Justice's office.

"Do you have an appointment?"

"Yes, ma'am. John Atwood and Sarah Johnson at nine for a marriage ceremony."

"Ah, yes. I see you on the list. There's one couple ahead of you. They're with him now. Are these two little darlin's going to be your witnesses?"

"If it were legal they would be," said John. He ruffled Katy's hair. She pulled away and straightened her hair, eyes shooting daggers at her father for messing it up.

The other couple came out, hand in hand, smiles on their faces. Sarah wished she and John were as happy about getting married. Maybe someday that would be them. Walking down the street holding hands.

"Are we ready?" The judge's voice brought her back to the present.

"We are, your honor," said John.

"Let's begin. Dearly beloved, we are

gathered here in the presence of…."

Sarah barely listened until she heard her name, "Do you Sarah Jane Johnson take this man to be your lawfully wedded husband? To have and to hold; for richer or for poorer; through sickness and in health from this day forward as long as you both shall live?"

"I do." Her hands shook as she placed the plain gold band on his finger. It was too small. She'd bought it in Chicago and would have to get it resized for him.

"Do you John Robert Atwood take this woman as your lawfully wedded wife? To have and to hold; for richer or for poorer; through sickness and in health from this day forward as long as you both shall live?"

"I do." John slid a small gold band with five small diamond chips in it on her finger. It was beautiful and felt cool against her skin.

"Then by the power vested in me by the Governor of the Colorado Territory, I pronounce you man and wife. You may kiss the bride."

John took her face gently in both of his hands, leaned down and gave her the sweetest kiss she'd ever known. Sarah flushed at the promise in the kiss. MaryAnn giggled and Katy smiled, taking MaryAnn's hand.

"Thank you, Judge," said John. "What do I owe you?"

"That's two dollars, Mr. Atwood. I wish you and Mrs. Atwood a happy future."

"Thank you, sir. I'm sure it will be," replied Sarah.

"Well, ladies, shall we head home

now?" asked John.

Katy nodded vigorously.

"Yes," said MaryAnn and Sarah simultaneously.

Sarah laughed. Katy still held MaryAnn's hand and Sarah brought both girls into a big hug. "Let's go home. We have a new life beginning for all of us.

Katy tugged on MaryAnn's hand and the two girls skipped all the way back to the buckboard and forward into the future.

CHAPTER 3

The trip to the ranch took them through gently rolling hills covered in bright green grass and fields full of wildflowers bursting with the colors of the rainbow. A freight train passed them headed to Golden City, the territorial capital of the Colorado Territory, to drop off supplies for the mining towns of Central City and Black Hawk, which according to John were up Clear Creek Canyon from Golden City. The train only carried supplies to Golden City and usually gold, cattle, and farm goods back to Denver. It didn't carry passengers or Sarah would have taken it all the way. Passenger service stopped in Denver.

The road was well traveled and wide enough for two wagons. They passed several headed toward Denver. Some of them carried families, others only freight. One carried gold. John said he could tell by the six armed men that accompanied it.

Sarah asked, "Do they get robbed often?"

"Not with a guard like that. Outlaws would have to be crazy or really desperate to try it."

"Do you have many outlaws here? Is it something I should be aware of?"

"Nah, we don't get that kind of trouble out here. They stick to the cities. I have ten men working for me, so we're safe from just about anything. I've been having one stay with Katy while I'm out working but now you're here and can take over those duties. I also have a cook and housekeeper, though I'm hoping you can cook, because she's terrible and will be the first one to tell you so. Her name is Bertha."

"Of course, I'll watch the girls. Katy and MaryAnn seem to get along well. And yes, I can cook. I just hope the trunk that's missing doesn't have my recipes in it. If it does, then the meals I fix are going to be on the simple side."

"None of us mind simple. We're just looking for edible."

Sarah laughed. "Well, they will definitely be edible."

She looked back at the girls. Katy

still held MaryAnn's hand while MaryAnn chattered away. Katy nodded or shook her head in response to her questions and she had a million of them.

"Do you have a horse of your own? Can I ride it?"

Katy nodded twice in answer. It seemed to be enough for MaryAnn. She treated Katy as she did everyone. Like a new friend. It didn't matter that Katy didn't talk. MaryAnn talked enough for the both of them.

They passed through Golden City. The little city was nestled in a valley between the foothills of the Rockies and a flat plateau. John said his ranch was about three miles northwest of town.

Before she knew it they were pulling off the main road through a gate that read *J*

Bar A Ranch. She could see buildings about half a mile down the road. As they got closer she made out seven different structures. She recognized the house and the barn. What the others were, she didn't know yet.

"The house. It's larger than I thought it would be. And I assume the big red building is the barn. What are the others?"

"There's the ice house, smoke house, chicken coop, bunk house, that's where the cowboys live, and the outhouse"

Alarmed, Sarah asked, "You don't have running water?"

"There's a hand pump in the kitchen but we don't have an indoor bathroom."

"Oh, dear."

He patted her on the knee. "It'll be fine. You'll get used to it."

"I'm sure I will."

Sarah watched as he flushed a little.

"I'm sorry," he said. "I probably should have let you know that compared to what you're used to we're going to seem a mite primitive."

She shook her head. "I admit I hadn't expected it to be quite so spartan, but I'm undaunted."

"That's a girl. You've got some spunk. I like that." He gave her knee a little squeeze.

No one had ever said Sarah had spunk. She'd always let life run her over. Now she was grasping it around the neck and hanging on for the ride.

There'd been plenty of time to think on the train out here. She'd gone over everything she'd been through, everything she'd done. She wouldn't change any of it because she had her beautiful MaryAnn. Everything was worth it to have her.

Now there was a chance for happiness she'd never dare to hope for in New York. A home and family of her own. She had both now. She looked at her new home. It was a beautiful, two story, white washed, wood structure. There was a large porch on the front facing east. Sunrise should be spectacular.

John pulled the buckboard to a stop in front of the porch. He jumped down, came around to her side and reached up for her. She placed her hands on his broad shoulders and he grasped her around the waist and lifted her down. Breathless, she stepped away. Then he got each of the girls.

Katy ran inside with MaryAnn on her

heels. Sarah and John followed at a more sedate pace.

The layout of the house was as simple inside as outside. They walked into the parlor which ran the width of the house. The stairs were on the far right side. Leading out of the parlor was a hall. On one side was the dining room and John's office. The other side had the kitchen, pantry and a bedroom for the housekeeper, Bertha.

When they entered the kitchen there was a large, gray haired woman sitting at the table shelling peas for the evening meal. Three dead chickens sat on the counter waiting to be plucked.

"Bertha, this is Mrs. Atwood," said John by way of introduction

"Sarah. Please call me Sarah." She extended her hand in greeting.

Bertha wiped her floured, calloused hands on her apron and shook Sarah's with both of hers. "Real glad to meet you, Mrs. Atwood…Sarah. Real glad. You can cook can't you? Mr. Atwood said he was pretty sure you could. I don't cook real good. Don't like it. So I'm hopin' you can, 'cause we all need some good vittles."

"Yes, Bertha," Sarah laughed. "I can cook, but I'll need your help learning my way around the kitchen and with prep. For instance, I have no idea what to do with a chicken like that." She pointed at the counter. "I've never plucked a chicken in my life. Our cook always did that."

"Don't you worry none about that. I can pluck a chicken in my sleep. I'll get 'em all ready so all you got to do is fix 'em."

Sarah smiled. She and Bertha were

going to get along famously.

"Now that you two have met, I'm going to take Sarah upstairs and show her the rest of the house."

"I heard Katy running up the stairs. She made enough noise for two people."

Sarah and John laughed. "That's because there were two people. Sarah's little girl, MaryAnn, is with Katy."

Bertha smiled, revealing a small gap between her front teeth. "Well now I'm glad to hear it. Katy has needed a friend to play with."

"So has MaryAnn. They're both only children, but they seem to have made friends with each other," said Sarah.

"Come on, I'll show you the upstairs and get your trunks in here so you can start unpacking. And we'll see what our two special girls are up to."

"Plotting our demise no doubt," said Sarah.

John barked out a laugh. She liked when he laughed. His dimples showed and he didn't seem so intimidating.

They went upstairs.

"Up here are only bedrooms. Someday I want to put water and a bathroom up here but that's on down the road. Katy's bedroom is the first on the right. I thought we could put MaryAnn across the hall. The back left bedroom can be the nursery. Our bedroom is the back right."

He opened the door and stepped aside so she could go into their room before him. It was a big room. She walked around touching everything. There was a double bed, tall boy dresser, small commode with a pitcher and basin on it, two nightstands, an overstuffed chair by the large picture window and a changing screen in the corner with a chamber pot behind it.

"That's a beautiful screen. One of Dorothy's touches?"

"Yes, but you can removed it if you like. If there's anything you don't like I'll have it taken away."

Sarah touched his hand. "It's fine. The room is lovely. Dorothy had good taste. After all, she married you."

John cleared his throat. "Yes, she did didn't she?"

She looked everything over and then came back to the bed. Amazing how a double bed can look so small. She swallowed hard. John was going to want a wedding night. How was she going to explain that she didn't really know what she was supposed to do? She'd only made love once before and that brought about MaryAnn.

"It's a lovely room."

"Like I said, you can change whatever you like. It's your room now, too."

"Thank you."

"The chair by the window is for reading. Do you like to read?"

Sarah tore her gaze away from the bed. "I'm sorry, what?"

"I was asking if you liked to read. Dorothy did, so I put the chair there by the window. She didn't get to make much use of it. There's a lot of work to running a successful ranching operation. Not much time left for anything else."

"I'm sure there is. I…um…yes, I do

like to read."

"Are you nervous, Sarah?"

She heard laughter in his voice and glanced up at him. Too late she saw his eyes smoldering.

"I…I am a little nervous." She turned away from him, walked to the closet and opened the door. Maybe she could just walk in close the door and disappear.

"You don't need to be."

She looked back at him. His hands were behind his back. She could see his erection straining at his pants. "I don't?"

He shook his head. "How long has it been since you made love?"

"Since before MaryAnn was born. Her father died at Bull Run. She never knew her father. He and I were…."

He walked over to her and placed two

fingers gently against her lips. "You're rambling." He replaced his fingers with his lips. Soft, firm lips. He didn't touch her except with his lips. She wrapped her arms around his neck and brought him closer. His tongue pressed against the seam of her lips and she opened for him. Warm, he tasted clean and he smelled so good and she couldn't get close enough. Finally he brought his arms around her and gathered her close. She'd missed this. Kissing. A man's touch. A….

"Hee hee," came MaryAnn's little giggle.

She and John broke apart, looked over to the door and saw both little girls laughing.

Sarah knew she flushed and it was confirmed when MaryAnn said, "Did Mr. Atwood make you hot again, Mama?

You're all red."

She wanted the floor to just swallow her up. When she looked at John, he had a big grin on his face.

"I make you hot, do I?"

"Oh, just hush." She went to the door and shoo'd the girls out of the room. "Let's go see if there are any cookies. Or better yet, let's go make some." A low chuckle followed her out of the room. She didn't look back.

*****

"Bertha, do we have the makings for sugar cookies?"

She and the girls walked into the kitchen. Bertha had just finished plucking the chickens and was working on the pin feathers with a small pair of pliers.

"I'm sure there is. I don't bake much.

Even worse at it than I am at cooking. Look at you. The boss got a good one with you. A looker who can cook and bake, too."

"Stop. You'll make me blush."

"Too late," came a deep, baritone from behind her. He put his hand on her waist and gave her a small hug. Now she knew she was blushing. She had to get over this or she'd be forever red.

She swatted at him. "Now stop that."

The girls and Bertha laughed.

"I know when I'm not wanted. I'll go get your trunks while you do some cooking."

"We're making cookies," she called to his retreating form.

"Mama, do you like Mr. Atwood?"

Sarah looked down at the little girls. Both were looking up at her with such serious faces.

"Yes, I do like Mr. Atwood." She watched both of them visibly relax. "Why?"

"Well, me and Katy, we like each other and if you didn't like Mr. Atwood we might not stay."

"Whoa, right there. We are *not* going anywhere. This is our home now. Forever."

"Forever," echoed John from the kitchen door. "Katydid. No one is going to take Sarah and MaryAnn from us. We all belong to each other now."

"That's right," confirmed Sarah.

"I put the first of the trunks in our bedroom. Do you want the other two there too?"

"No, put them in MaryAnn's room. I'll unpack them from there and we won't be tripping over them while I do it. I have to figure out what trunk got misplaced. Maybe I'll get lucky and it'll be the one with the spring clothes in it."

He nodded and started to leave. "Are you girls alright now?"

"Yes, sir," answered MaryAnn. Katy nodded.

"Good." He left to get the rest of the trunks.

"I sure am glad you like him, Mama."

"Me, too, sweetheart. You girls want to help me make cookies?"

They both nodded.

"Bertha, where are the dish towels. These little helpers need aprons. And so do I."

"Coming right up, missus."

Sarah lit the oven, mixed the cookie dough and rolled it out. The girls took turns cutting it out and putting it on the cookie sheet. While they baked she cut the chicken up for frying and heated the grease on the stove. After ten minutes, she checked the cookies. They needed a few more minutes so she put the chicken in for frying. When she'd gotten all of it in the two cast iron Dutch ovens, the cookies were ready to come out.

She took the cookies and put them on a dish towel to cool while she put another batch in the oven. The girls each got a warm cookie and a glass of cold milk from the ice box.

"What is that wonderful smell?" asked John as he came into the kitchen rolling down his shirt sleeves.

She smiled at him. Her heart did a little flip. Oh my, look at those arms. "*That* is sugar cookies. Would you like one?"

"Aren't you afraid it'll spoil my dinner?"

"The way I cook, nothing is going to spoil your dinner. Which reminds me," she went and turned the chicken over.

"That smells good, too. What are you making for dinner?"

"Fried chicken, biscuits, mashed potatoes, and fresh peas that Bertha shelled. We'll have sugar cookies for dessert. How does that sound?"

"Great. I put the trunks where you wanted them."

"Thank you, I'll start unpacking after dinner."

Sarah and Bertha set the large, rectangular, kitchen table and Bertha banged the triangle calling all the men to supper.

There was a small porch off the kitchen. Bertha placed a couple of basins of hot water and several towels on a table there so the men could wash up before meals. They washed their face and hands before coming in to eat.

"Men," said John, "this is Sarah, my new wife. She is also our new cook, no offense to Bertha."

"None taken, boss. I'm glad to be rid of the chore and am looking forward to some good vittles like everybody else."

He turned back to the men. "You will show Sarah and our daughter MaryAnn the same honor and respect you did Dorothy and do Katy. Dig in everyone."

She was somewhat surprised at their good manners. They were all respectful and calmly passed the food around the table.

Even though there was a dining room they didn't use it. The family and the hired help all ate together. Sarah liked that.

The men were very animated after the first bite. There were ooh's and ah's and then silence as they began to eat in earnest. There were no leftovers either. Sarah made a mental note to cook more. The men would have eaten it if she'd cooked it. They worked hard. They needed their strength.

There was almost a scuffle over the last biscuit. Bertha stopped it by taking it herself.

"Thank you for a fine meal, Mrs. Atwood," said Ben, one of the drovers.

"Thank you," the other men echoed.

"That was the best meal we've had in two years," said Bertha. "You did real good, boss. She's a definite keeper."

John smiled. “I couldn’t agree more.”

“Thank you all, but it was nothing really.”

“Nothing? Talent is not nothing and you have a definite talent for cooking. Bertha you are officially retired from the cook position,” said John.

Sara wasn’t used to such praise and gloried in it.

“Let’s clean up now. You girls can help by bringing the dishes to the sink,” said Sarah.

“You never mind about the dishes.” Bertha filled a metal bucket with water and set it on the stove to heat. “I’ll clean up. You go and unpack. I know you can’t have done any of it.”

“Thank you, I think I will. In the mean time, I want you girls to get ready for a bath and then to bed."

"Ah, Mama, do we got to take a bath?"

Sarah looked over both girls, still in their finery from earlier today. Neither one was messy or dirty.

"Okay, you don't have to bathe tonight but for sure tomorrow. Now go on upstairs and put your nightgowns on. I'll be up in a little bit to tuck you in."

She finished clearing the table to Bertha's grumblings and then went upstairs to MaryAnn's room. Her empty room. She went across the hall to Katy's room and found both little girls fast asleep in Katy's bed.

"Looks like they've decided to share a room," said John from behind her.

"I guess so."

"Do you mind?"

"Not at all. I think they need each other and I'm glad they're friends." Sarah closed the door to Katy's room.

"Me, too. I have high hopes Katy will start talking again with MaryAnn here."

"I hope you're right. It would be wonderful. Do you think the outlaw threatened her or something like that?"

"I don't know. I hope not. Now come along. Time for us to go to bed, too." He put his arm around her waist and guided her to their room. "I know you're a little nervous, Sarah, but I won't hurt you. I won't even make love to you tonight but I will hold you and touch you and look at you. It's been more than two years since I've made love and I'm a little rusty."

"I haven't found my nightgown yet.

I'll have to look through the trunk in our room."

"No need."

"No need?"

"Yup. I want you naked as the day you were born. I want us to get used to each other's body. Are you willing to try it? I won't force you."

She put her hand on top of his and moved into his embrace, her back to his chest. "I'd like that. Getting to know each other slowly."

"Yes." He turned her in his arms and finished the kiss the girls interrupted earlier. "Now that was a proper kiss."

Proper! Her knees were weak, barely capable of keeping her upright and there was warmth down in her center. An ache so deep inside she would have thought she was sick if she didn't remember a similar ache once before. A very long time back. A lifetime ago.

They went into the bedroom and John began shucking his clothes. Sarah unbuttoned her jacket and put it on top of the trunk. Then came her skirt followed by her blouse. She stood there in her chemise and bloomers.

"Turn around Sarah. I want to see you," he said from the bed where he laid in all his God given glory.

She took a deep breath and let it out again as she turned. He was magnificent. Hard muscle covered his arms and torso. She tried to pass over his groin but was drawn to it like a duck to water. He was fully erect and monstrous in size compared to Lee.

"Don't be shy. You're a beautiful woman."

Bolstered by his praise she took off her chemise.

John sucked in his breath. "Beautiful doesn't begin to describe you. Exquisite is better."

Fortified, she dropped her bloomers and stood before him totally naked. Stripped of all the barriers she'd had for most of her life.

CHAPTER 4

"Now come to bed."

She walked to her side of the bed and turned down the covers.

"No. Not yet. Don't get under the covers."

"But I'm cold."

"Come here. I'll warm you up." He lifted his left arm in invitation.

She took a deep fortifying breath and moved close to him. Felt his skin on hers, hot, almost burning.

His arm closed around her, bringing her closer, flattening her breasts against him.

"This isn't so bad, is it? You're warmer now?"

"Yes, this is nice and I am warmer." She draped her arm across his belly, then started to run her fingers through the soft curly hair on his chest. There wasn't a lot, just a dusting.

His hand went to her butt. He caressed her then moved up her side. Gently, he pushed her back onto the bed and away from his body. Lowering his head he gave her a kiss. "So soft." He murmured.

She closed her eyes and kissed him back. The ache between her legs got more intense.

He moved his lips to her neck and then worked his way lower finally stopping at her breast.

"You have the most beautiful breasts. See how your nipples pebble for me. Begging for my mouth. Never let it be said that I made a woman beg." With those words he lowered his mouth to her nipple and laved it with his tongue.

Her head fell back into the fresh pillow and she arched her back to get him closer.

He raised his head, her nipple popping out of his mouth. "Like that do you?"

"God, yes." She felt moisture between her legs and wanted him to come into her and ease the ache that built more intensely with each of his ministrations.

Chuckling he turned his attention to her other nipple. He suckled and gently bit it.

She nearly came off the bed. The pleasure wonderful. She crushed his head to her with both her hands. Her feet rubbed along his naked, well muscled thighs

He lifted his head and let go of her nipple with a delicious pop and then worked his way down her body, circling her belly button with his tongue and then stabbing it.

She could barely breathe, and then he was there, where she wanted him, nudging her legs apart.

"Look how much you want me," he said and smiled up at her. Then he dropped his head between her legs and his tongue was on her.

"Oh my God. John!" Pleasure streaked through her body from head to toe.

He tongued her little nub of pleasure and then sucked her. The next thing she knew she was soaring, shattered into a million pieces. He licked her softly, soothing her, staying with her as she returned to earth.

She was back. Her body limp, spent. "That was amazing."

His hand smoothed over her belly back to her breast. It was followed by his lips. He worked his way up until he was over her again, "You're beautiful. Amazing." Then he kissed her.

She opened her mouth for him and the ache started building again. She wrapped her arms around him. Pulling back, she looked into his brown eyes, now black with passion. "Come into me. Please, John. Don't make me wait."

"You're sure?"

She smiled and nodded. "More sure

than I've ever been of anything."

He smiled back at her and raised himself over her and between her legs. She felt him at her opening. He entered her, slowly.

"Christ, you're tight. It's like it's your first time."

"It's been a long time. You don't mind do you? We can stop if you would rather."

"Never. I couldn't stop now if I wanted to." With those words he pulled out and then back in farther up her slick passage. Out again and he slammed into her, buried himself all the way. Then he stopped. Let her adjust to him before he started moving again.

She matched his motions, pushing up when he pushed in and pulling back when he did.

Faster and faster he moved, then he groaned, buried his face in her neck and spent himself inside of her. He laid on her breathing hard.

Her hands moved of their own volition to his back and she hugged him to her.

They stayed like that for a while until his breathing came back to normal then he lifted off of her and lay back taking her with him.

"That was amazing. Forgive me for not attending to you. It's been a long time for me and obviously for you too. If I didn't know you had a child I would have thought it was your first time."

"I told you that I haven't made love since before MaryAnn was born. Well, the truth is, I only made love that one time. Her father was called up unexpectedly and we only had the one time. That was all it took for me to get my MaryAnn."

"No wonder you're so tight. You're basically a virgin. That's not bad."

"You don't mind?"

"Good grief, no. I feel honored to be able to teach you about lovemaking. And I believe you're going to be a good student."

"Because I have a good teacher?"

"Flattery will get you…everywhere."

She smiled and took a deep breath. "This is nice. Laying here together and talking afterwards."

"It is. But now is the time for sleep. Tomorrow comes early." He got up and put out the kerosene lamp.

Sarah rolled away to her side of the

bed and got under the covers. Even with them over her, she felt cold and bereft.

John got back in bed, moved over and spooned with her, his arm gathering her close.

She sighed. Content.

*****

She awoke to kisses on the side of her cheek.

"There you are. Awake at last. It's time to get up and start the day."

"It's still night."

"Not on a ranch. Work starts for me and the men at daybreak. You need to get cooking breakfast. Now don't turn over and go back to sleep." He grabbed the covers and tore them off her.

She turned over and grabbed them trying to bring them back up.

"Oh no, you don't." He swatted her on the butt. "Get up. You have to find clothes to wear remember."

Sitting up on the side of the bed she yawned and then stood. "You're right. Luckily this is my trunk and there should be something in it close to the top that I can wear." She got up and put on her bloomers and chemise, ever mindful that he watched her every move. "You're staring at me like a starving man and I'm your next meal."

"You are my next meal. The only meal for which I hunger."

She knew she blushed, but there was something about the man that kept her hot and flushed all the time. She could easily fall in love with him. Maybe already had. But now she needed to get dressed and out before she begged him to make love to her again.

Out of the trunk she pulled a black skirt and pink and white striped shirtwaist blouse. It would serve her well for the work she had in front of her today. She would get breakfast on and then sit down with Bertha to discuss a schedule for the housework.

Breakfast for fifteen people is no small affair especially when eleven of those are hardworking men who need a lot of food to sustain them. She started off with eggs and biscuits, bacon and sausage, pancakes with jam and butter, oatmeal, and finally coffee. All of them ate like they were starving. There was not a scrap left over when they were done.

After breakfast, she started a pot of beans with the ham she found in the larder. She asked Bertha to peel potatoes, turnips and carrots for a beef stew. She'd leave these on the stove for the men to eat when they took breaks. She also made another batch of biscuits and some cornbread. Then she started on the dessert baking. She'd checked the pantry and the cellar for fruit and found some canned peaches and blueberries. They'd be perfect for pies and a couple of cobblers. Some for supper tonight and some for breakfast tomorrow. At the rate these people ate, she was going to have to make a trip to town for supplies.

She wondered if John would be able to take her since she didn't know how to drive a team yet. Or maybe she and Bertha could go if Bertha could drive. They could take the girls and make an outing of it.

John told her he'd be working in the barn for most of the day so she walked out there.

The barn was painted a dull red and had big double doors on both ends. This end also had a regular door which she entered through, thankful she didn't have to try and open the big doors.

"John. John are you here?" she called out.

"Sarah?" came the voice from above.

She looked up and saw him standing in the loft. "What are you doing up there?"

"Working. Moving Hay. What are you doing down here?"

"I came to ask you a question. Can you come down so we don't have to shout?"

"Sure. Give me a minute."

He disappeared from view and Sarah started looking around her. There were five good sized stalls. In one of them were a mother horse and her baby.

“Oh, aren’t you just adorable,” she said when the baby came to investigate. With his mother so close he was emboldened and sniffed at Sarah’s open hand.

“Here give him a little sugar. You’ll have a friend for life.”

“Oh!” Sarah jumped back. “You startled me.”

“Sorry. Here,” he placed a sugar cube in her hand. “Give the colt the cube. He also likes carrots and apples if you’re so inclined.”

“Here boy,” Sarah urged him, then held the sugar cube in her fingers.

“Flatten your hand and put the cube on it. He could bite your fingers the other way and we don’t want that.”

She did as he said and the little colt came over, sniffed then brushed her hand with his soft lips as he scooped up the treat.

"His lips are so soft."

"Not as soft as someone else's I know." His eyes were dark and she knew if she wanted they'd make love right then and there. She glanced down and saw that he was definitely ready.

"You have to stop that. I'm in a perpetual state of embarrassment. My daughter thinks I'm suffering from the heat because I'm red all the time."

"So?"

"So? It's your fault."

"Really? Why is that do you suppose?"

"I don't know. I've never had this response to anyone before. I don't normally blush."

"You don't?" He crossed his arms and leaned up against the stall door. "Just with me?"

"Yes."

"Good. I'm glad to hear it. I'd hate to think you were sexually attracted to other men."

"What?! I'm not…."

"Yes, you are. I knew the minute you blushed the first time."

"Awfully sure of yourself," she teased.

"Yes. I am." He pushed away from the stall and took her in his arms. His lips found hers for a scorching kiss. "When it comes to reading you."

She hoped that wasn't true. She hadn't been completely truthful with him about her background. Oh, she'd never actually lied with words, but she lied by omission. But surely, Mrs. Selby told him. A little voice in her head said that probably wasn't true. She hadn't shared the fact that Katy was so traumatized by her mother's murder that she refused to speak. That was different, she told herself. Different than being a fallen woman.

Closing her eyes she chased the doubt away.

He pulled back but kept his hands locked behind her back. "What did you need before I so rudely interrupted you?"

"You weren't rude." She leaned back allowing him to support her and put her hands on his shoulders. "But what I wanted was to see if someone can take me to town for supplies. I need food stuffs if I'm going to feed us decently."

"Make me a list and I'll have Bertha go."

"Well, I thought maybe the girls and I could go with her and make an outing of it. I understand a lot of farmers bring their produce to town and it would be good for the girls. And I could get to know the suppliers."

"I'd rather the girls stay here. I'm not ready for Katy to go to town without me. She might see the outlaw. They don't always were masks you know. She could go even deeper into trauma if I'm not there to protect her."

"I hadn't thought about that. I'm sorry, I should have thought about Katy's safety first."

"You're new at this. You haven't had

to think about MaryAnn's safety in the same way. Besides that, the girls are just fine here. They're getting along and learning how to play with one another." He thought about it for a minute. "What about this? You go with Bertha and get what you need for a couple of weeks. Then I'll take you and the girls next time."

"That sounds fine. It would be even better if you taught me to drive a team so I could go by myself when I need to."

"I can do that. How about one day next week after breakfast?"

"Wonderful. When we go, if the produce is any good I'll buy enough to can. Do you know if there are canning supplies anywhere? I doubt that Bertha has done any canning but Dorothy must have. I found some lovely peaches and blueberries in the cellar."

"Did you check the pantry or the cupboards in the kitchen?"

"No. I thought I'd check with you as long as I was asking things."

"I don't know where they'd be. If you can't find any, buy some at the mercantile." He unclasped his hands from around her waist and she let go of his shoulders. "I should get back to work."

"Me, too. I have to get dinner cooking. Do you have any requests for supper?"

"Whatever you fix will be wonderful. The men have been congratulating me on marrying well because of your cooking skills. You've made the two best meals we've had in years. Poor Bertha, she tried but it just isn't something she's good at."

"I'm glad they like me for something."

"I like you for something," he waggled his eyebrows and winked at her.

"Oh my." She knew she blushed again.

He laughed.

She turned and walked out of the barn, fanning herself as she went, his laughter followed her. She smiled.

*****

Sarah finished with the breakfast dishes. She'd washed and Bertha rinsed and dried. Today was her first lesson in driving a team. She ran upstairs and checked her appearance in the mirror. She was going to spend some time alone with John that wasn't in bed. Though she couldn't complain about that. He was a very caring, generous lover.

She always climaxed at least once. Usually more.

She pushed stray tendrils of hair back up into the knot on top of her head. It probably wouldn't stay but no one could say she hadn't tried. If she'd been back in New York she wouldn't have dared to step out of the bedroom much less the house with a hair out of place. Aunt Gertrude would turn over in her grave if she saw Sarah now.

She ran down the stairs and out on to the front porch. John waited in the buggy, the smallest of their conveyances. As soon as he saw her he jumped down and came around to help her up into the seat. Then he went around and got back in.

"Okay. You ready?"

"Yes." She could barely breathe; excitement about learning to drive was the least of her worries. Being this close to her husband and them both having clothes on was almost sexier than without. Almost.

She smiled up at him. "What do I do first?"

He handed her the reins. "First you take off the hand brake. I'm going to do it this time, but when you're driving you'll be in my seat and you'll set it and release it. Always remember to set it. It won't stop the horses from taking off if they were determined but it serves as a reminder to them they aren't supposed to move."

"Right. Brake."

"Next you take the reins and give them a little flick of the wrist to swat the horses butt."

She tried but wasn't doing it right because the horses didn't move so much as an inch.

He took them from her, “like this.” He jerked his wrists and the leather straps went up and came back down on the horses rumps and they started walking. “Now if you want them to go faster lift them and bring them back down and say ‘giddyup’.”

She nodded. “Giddyup.”

“Okay you try it.” He handed the reins back to her.

She slapped the them on the animals rumps and they started trotting.

“Good. Now turn them to the right.”

“How?”

“Pull on the right rein while leaving the left one alone. Just the right.”

She did and was surprised the horses actually went right like she wanted them to.

“I think you’ve got it. When you

want them to go left pull on the left rein. Want them to stop, pull back on both reins together."

"This is easy. Thank you for taking the time to teach me. I know it probably put you behind in your work today."

"Not really. I'm taking the morning off to show you around the ranch. Give me the reins and we'll go."

She handed them back to him. He swatted the horses rumps and got them into a slow canter. A much smoother gait for pulling a buggy.

They drove west up to the mouth of a small canyon and then went into it. Traveling where there was no road, it was a little on the bumpy side and Sarah grabbed John's arm when it got to be too much.

Shortly, John stopped the buggy. She

noticed that he not only set the brake, he hobbled the horses as well. “I don’t want to get stranded up here if they get spooked for some reason.”

He grabbed a blanket from the rear of the buggy and they walked a short way to a small stream. It was clear and looked only inches deep. “Oh, can we wade, it’s so shallow.”

“It’s deceiving because it’s so clear and running pretty slow now, but you get away from the bank and it gets midway up your thighs.”

He placed the blanket on the ground. Then he bowed and swept his arm toward the blanket. “My, Lady.”

Sarah flushed and sat arranging her skirt around her. “Oh my, aren’t we the gallant one.”

"I brought you here for nefarious purposes."

"Oh, what is that?"

"I intend to take advantage of you."

"Here? Out in the open?"

He smiled and undid his gun belt dropping it on the edge of the blanket.

Sarah scooted over when he came down on his knees next to her.

He reached up and caressed her jaw with his hand then ran his finger down her neck to the top button of her blouse and undid it. Moving slowly he undid the next and the next, revealing her an inch at a time until her shirt lay completely open. Then he did the same thing with the ties on her chemise. She sat there mesmerized by the desire in his eyes. He leaned forward and took her lips with his. His gentle touch sent goosebumps to her skin and heat to her core.

She leaned up and undid the top button of his shirt, exposing him as slowly as he did her. When she finally had it open she pulled it from his pants, slid it down over his shoulders and his arms until he was free of the encumbrance to her exploration. She ran her hands over his firm chest muscles, stopping to tweak his nipples as he so often did hers.

They both rid themselves of their shoes and bottoms. When they were both naked, John said to her, "lie back on the blanket. Let me pleasure you."

Shaking her head she asked him, "Can't I enjoy you as you do me? With my mouth?"

He got very still. "Are you sure? Most women don't like to do that for their man."

"I don't know if I'll like it or not. I've never done it. Lie back."

He did as she asked. His erection hard as steel just at the mention of this act.

She leaned down and tentatively took him in her mouth. Just a little way. She ran her tongue around the tip, feeling the silk of his skin over the hard rod beneath. He amazed her. This was such a unique part of him. The softness and the strength combined. She took him farther into her mouth and then back out while her hand explored the sacs below his staff. They were different. The skin wrinkled and loose compared to his shaft.

Around and around with her tongue, then she licked the underside of his penis and he groaned. She liked the power this gave her. He was hers to do with as she pleased. Or so she thought.

Suddenly he grasped her hair and brought her face up to his.

"I need in you now."

He rolled her over onto her back, reared back and plunged into her with no preamble, no preparation. It didn't matter she was slick and ready for him as she always was.

Two, three pumps into her and he groaned again and buried his face in her neck. She felt his hot release inside her. Each time she hoped she would get pregnant. She wanted children with this man. Falling hard, hell, she'd already fallen head over heels in love with her husband. She only wished he felt the same.

They lay there wrapped in each

other's arms for she didn't know how long. Long enough that she could suddenly feel the chill air as the sweat from their exertions dried. She shivered.

"We should get dressed and get back," he said. "I still have work to do and so do you."

"This was nice. Thank you for bringing me here."

"Thank you for giving of yourself so generously."

"I liked it. You feel amazing. I never knew."

He chuckled. "You are a wonder. How did I get so lucky?"

"I was just thinking the same thing."

He kissed her, then turned and grabbed his drawers and pants. She stood and put on her bloomers and chemise.

“I wish we could stay here all day. Go wading and have a picnic. Just you, me and nature.”

“One day we will. I’ll make time and you can plan the meals so they’re easy enough that even Bertha can’t mess them up.”

“That I can do. You just let me know when you can get away for the whole day.”

He gave her a kiss that sizzled her all the way to her toes and made her want to start all over. “It’s a deal.”

*****

They were getting closer. She felt it. She’d been there for a month and John made love to her every night, but she couldn’t break that barrier between them. His wife’s ghost haunted them. Haunted him.

He’d told her after their first week

together, "Don't fall in love with me Sarah. I can't love you back. I'll never love anyone again. It's too painful."

She would change his mind. He would come to love her. If she just did everything he wanted he'd love her. She knew it. She just had to make it happen.

*****

June 25, 1867

William Grayson boarded the west bound train. Sarah had been gone for more than a month in the wild frontier. She should be more than willing to return with him to the comforts of New York where she'd have servants to do everything for her.

Everything he'd read about the west said it was quite primitive. No running water, no bathrooms, no servants. The photo's showed tired, dirty people, old before their time. He was sure Sarah didn't want to live like that.

Well, that was not going to be Sarah's fate. He'd bring her back, get her marriage annulled and marry her himself. He had it all worked out. She'd be glad to see him and beg for him to take her back.

In eight days all his dreams would be coming true and Sarah would be his.

*****

A buckboard drove slowly up the road to the house. It was piled high with luggage and trunks of varying shapes and sizes. The driver pulled up in front of the house.

"What can I do for you, mister?" asked John from the top of the porch steps.

"I'm looking for a Sarah Johnson. Would this be the correct place?"

"It is."

"Good. I'm from the Denver Pacific Railway. We found Mrs. Johnson's trunk.

"Oh, good." Sarah said from behind him. "The new clothes for the girls and most importantly my recipes."

"Recipes?"

"From my old cook in New York. I wrote down each of her recipes. I think tonight we'll have roast beef with Yorkshire pudding. I swear you and the men will love it."

"I trust you. I'm sure we will."

"Can you sign here?" asked the driver shoving a piece of paper and pencil in John's direction.

"Sure." He put the paper on the porch rail and signed it and then handed it back to the driver. "Here you go."

"Thanks. You folks have a good day." The driver drove off to make other deliveries.

"What was that about clothes for the girls?"

"I bought clothes for MaryAnn in several larger sizes. Now that I have Katy too, they are for her as well."

"I'm sure they'll be tickled pink."

"Not as much as they were when you gave each of us a pair of pants to wear. I've never seen them so excited. I can barely get the two of them out of the pants long enough to wash them."

"Maybe you should wash the girls and the pants together," he said, smiling.

She laughed. "Now that's a definite possibility."

John carried the trunk inside and up to

MaryAnn's room.

CHAPTER 5

She put on the pants John bought her for riding. It was strangely liberating to wear them. Each of the girls had a pair as well. They looked so cute with their red plaid shirts and pigtails.

Sarah wore her green striped shirt and her hair in a long plait that reached to the middle of her back. John had also gotten her and MaryAnn boots. Katy already had a pair. She was tempted to wear them with her skirts too. They were much sturdier than her regular shoes and very comfortable.

She wasn't so sure it was a good idea, but the girls had been adamant that they come to her lesson, too. Well, MaryAnn had been adamant; Katy just grabbed her hand and pulled her down here.

"So, are you my student today?" John said, his voice full of amusement.

"If you laugh, I'm leaving right now." Her chin shot up and her back stiffened.

"I'm not laughing, love. I promise," he said around a smile.

He went over to a large gray horse. "This is Bertha. Don't laugh. Katy named her when she, Katy not the horse, was three. All of us including Bertha thought it was hysterical."

"You expect us to get on one of these monsters and stay on top while it moves.

And I don't understand why a little girl naming a gray horse after the gray haired cook would be funny. I'm sure I'll appreciate it more when I have all of this behind me."

He came over, took her by the hand and walked with her to the horse.

"Sarah meet Bertha. Take your hand and let her sniff it."

She did as he asked. Bertha smelled her then butted her hand with her head.

"She likes you. Scratch her behind the ears. That's right. See, she's just a big ol' softy."

"She's nice."

"And she's gentle. Come on let me help you up. Come around her head to the left side. I'm not sure what the original reason was for the left as opposed to the right. I think it had something to do with the sword being carried on the left side of the body. You couldn't mount a horse from the right side while wearing a sword. In any case the horse is broken to the left side mount."

She walked back to the left side where he stood.

"Now grab the saddle horn with both hands, put your left foot in the stirrup and pull yourself up. Then swing your right leg over the saddle.

She tried. She really did. She was barely able to reach the saddle horn. Trying to put her foot in the stirrup was impossible. She was too short.

Suddenly John's strong hands were at her waist, lifting her high. She fell face first over the saddle.

She yelled. “John I’m going to fall off.”

“No you’re not. I’ve got you.” He hadn’t released her, she was safe. She relaxed a bit.

“What do I do now?”

“I’m going to put your foot in the stirrup. Then you put your weight on that foot and stand up. Keep holding on to the saddle horn and swing your right leg over the top and sit on the saddle. Then put your right foot in the stirrup. You ready to try?”

She nodded and then realized he couldn’t see her. “Yes. I’ve got it.”

Following his instructions exactly she was amazed to find herself sitting up in the saddle.

“I did it.” Pleased with herself she grinned down at John.

He smiled back. "Good. Now take the reins in your right hand."

She did.

"That's right. Now punch your heels into her sides. This lets her know it's time to move."

Sarah lightly touched her boots to Bertha's side. She did nothing.

"You have to do it harder than that. She has to feel it and know you mean business."

She kicked her harder and Bertha started walking.

"Yahoo," Sarah yelled.

"Yay, Mama. You're riding."

"This is good but you can't walk everywhere." He swung up behind her. "Give me the reins." He took them and kicked Bertha in the sides. She started trotting and Sarah nearly fell off because of the hard uneven gait. The only thing that kept her in her seat was John's strong arms.

"Heeyah." He kicked Bertha again and she broke into a canter. This smoother gait actually made the ride fun and Sarah found herself enjoying it.

John kicked the horse again and she started galloping. This was her fastest gait and Sarah was exhilarated. She was free and laughed out loud.

He ran the horse as far as the gate at the main road, then slowed her down and turned around. The girls jumped up and down on their return.

"Our turn," MaryAnn called.

John dismounted first, then reached up and grasped Sarah around the waist and lifted her down. She slid down the front of his body and she gasped at the intimate contact.

"That was wonderful. I hope we do it again."

"You can count on it," he said before his lips claimed hers.

She wrapped her arms around his neck and kissed him back.

"Oh, yuck," said MaryAnn. "You two are mushy. I'm never getting married. There's too much kissing."

John and Sarah laughed. "Someday, you'll meet the right someone and you'll like all that kissing," said Sarah.

Katy made a face and MaryAnn said, "Nope. Never. We're never gonna do it."

John got back up on Bertha. "MaryAnn you get to ride first because you haven't done it before. Sarah, hand her up to me."

She lifted her up and John bent down and gathered her in his arms, then settled her on his lap.

He walked the horse a short way then took her up to a gallop. Sarah heard her daughter's laughter and smiled.

It was a very good day.

*****

July 4, 1867

It was Independence Day and Golden City was having a party. There was food and games and a rodeo in the afternoon. Farmers and ranchers from miles around came into town for the celebration.

"Come on ladies. Let's hurry it up," John called from the bottom of the stairs.

"Hold yer horses," said Bertha. She

was tying her bonnet as she walked to the stairs. "They's gettin' all prettied up for ya."

"We're ready," said Sarah from the head of the stairs.

She was a vision in pink. Her high-collared jacket buttoned up to her neck, hiding the bounty he knew was underneath. It nipped in at her small waist and flared over her skirt and the generous hips it covered. She'd done her hair up in a loose bun on top of her head and covered it all with a matching pink hat.

His daughters were visions of their own. Katy was in light blue with lace at the collar, the cuffs and the hem. She wore her best Sunday shoes and Sarah had braided her hair into long pigtails on the sides of her head. MaryAnn was in green. Her dress had ruffles at the bottom. Sarah had braided her hair in one long plait down her back.

He backed away and looked at all four of the females in his house. “You are all just beautiful. We’re taking the carriage today. Don’t plan on buying anything that has to come home. There’s just enough room for the five of us. And of course the three pies your mother made for the pot luck. Here. You each get to hold a pie. No nibbling!” A small smile escaped through his attempt to project a stern demeanor. He handed pies to Bertha, MaryAnn and Katy.

Katy nodded her head in agreement.

“Okay, Papa,” said MaryAnn.

Sarah beamed. It hadn’t taken MaryAnn very long to attach herself to John. She’d been needing a father all this time but Sarah hadn’t known just how much until

MaryAnn decided to call John 'Papa' after they'd been there only a week. It hadn't taken Sarah long to need John either. He was funny and kind, a gentle lover and very protective, not just of Katy, but of her and MaryAnn too.

John helped each of them into the carriage. MaryAnn first followed by Bertha and then Katy, all sat in the back. Then he helped Sarah in. Did his hands linger just a little longer on her waist or was it just her imagination making wishes?

If that was the case she had some other wishes. She wished they were alone so she could tell him what she'd just discovered herself that morning. She hadn't had her menses…she was pregnant, probably from the first time they made love. It seemed she was very fertile.

Tonight she'd tell him. Hopefully he'd be happy about it. No, she was sure he'd be happy. He doted on the girls. A baby would bring them all closer together. She wanted this baby so very much.

The carriage made good time and before long she was brought out of her reverie by the sight of Golden City. The streets were packed with pedestrians and vendor stalls. They'd closed off Main Street. Carriages, buckboards and buggies of all sizes were parked on the north end of town by the stable.

John pulled to a stop and put on the hand brake. Then he jumped down and helped each of them out. Sarah first. Did he feel the snugness of her skirt? Could he tell she was expanding?

"You girls go with Bertha and stay at

her side. Your mother and I will be along in a moment."

He turned back to her. "I just wanted a minute alone to kiss you and remind you that you're mine." He pulled her close and ravaged her mouth. "There's something different."

"John, I have something to tell you. I was going to wait until tonight but now is just as good."

"What is it?"

"I'm pregnant."

His eyes got wide and his eyebrows shot up. "Pregnant?!"

Sarah nodded.

He picked her up and swung her around in a circle. She wrapped her arms around his neck and hung on for dear life.

Their antics drew raised eyebrows

from some passersby. John didn't care. He shouted for the world to hear, "We're having a baby." Those same passersby now burst into applause.

"John let me down. John!"

"Alright." He lowered her to the ground then placed his hand gently on her stomach. "When?

"Near as I can tell, early February."

"February. That's not a lot of time."

"It's seven months. What do you need more time for?"

"I want to put water in the house. I've been meaning to do it for a while and always put it off but now…."

"That will be wonderful but," she pulled his hand, "now we need to tell our daughters."

They walked fast to catch up with

Bertha and the girls. They found them outside the ice cream parlor.

"Ah, just what I was wanting. How did you girls know?" asked John.

"We didn't but we're awful glad you did."

The five of them went inside. There was one table unoccupied. John sent Bertha and the kids to get it after getting their orders.

John and Sarah returned with the ice cream. "Chocolate for my girls and strawberry for Bertha. Your mother and I are sharing a scoop of chocolate and one of vanilla."

Everyone got quiet, concentrating on their treats.

"Are you going to tell them?" Sarah whispered.

"Tell us what, Mama?" asked MaryAnn.

"Well, it seems we are expecting a baby. You're going to have a little brother or sister. What do you think about that?"

MaryAnn leaned over and whispered something in Katy's ear. Katy nodded and then looked expectantly to John and Sarah.

"We think we'll like having a little brother or sister but what we'd really like is a puppy. Can we get one instead?"

John, Sarah and Bertha all laughed. So did some of the other customers.

"It's not a question of a puppy or a baby. We're having a baby," said Sarah.

Seeing their little faces filled with sorrow, John said, "Maybe we can get a puppy, too. *If* we find someone who has some to give away."

"Oh dear, boss, ya shouldn't a said that. We passed a farmer with pups to give away on the way here."

Katy and MaryAnn both smiled and nodded.

"Well, hell. I guess we take home a puppy."

They finished their ice cream and went in search of the farmer with the pups. They found him by the mercantile. He still had two puppies left. When the girls got sight of the two pups they took off running at the poor man.

Sarah noticed that the puppies each went to a different girl. MaryAnn and Katy both had big grins on their faces.

"John, can we get both pups? Did you see how they went to each girl? Like they knew them."

"I saw." He looked down at her. "I'm not going to win this one am I?"

"Nope."

"Then I guess we better take both dogs."

The farmer gave them a toothless grin. He tied short pieces of rope to each puppy's neck and handed the other end to the children.

"Now you just feed 'em scraps and they'll be just fine ya hear?" said the farmer.

"We will," said MaryAnn. "Thank you."

Katy nodded her thanks, too.

They all walked around visiting shops and farmer's stalls. The potluck kicked off at one o'clock. Sarah and the girls went back to the carriage to get the pies she'd made. The girls didn't want to go because they had to leave the puppies with John but Sarah made them. It was good for them to help out. They were old enough now.

When they got to the carriage, Sarah gave each of them a pie to carry. They'd started back and were nearing the stable when Katy suddenly dropped her pie and hid behind Sarah.

"Katy? What's the matter, love?" asked Sarah. "MaryAnn talk to her and see if you can understand what's the matter."

She went over to Katy. "What's wrong? Did you see something that scared you?"

Katy shook her head yes. She pointed toward the stable where several men were standing.

MaryAnn asked, "It's one of those men who scared you?"

Katy nodded her assent.

"Is he the man who killed your mama?" asked Sarah, suddenly realizing that would be the only reason Katy would be so scared now when she'd never been before.

She nodded and pointed to the men. One of them wore a bright red kerchief at his neck.

"Come on. Katy, stay on that side of me so you're hidden from him."

They walked as fast as they could. When they reached John and Bertha they were breathless.

Sarah and MaryAnn were talking at the same time, all of it coming out in a jumble.

Katy pulled on her father's pant leg. "Daddy!" she said.

Everyone quieted.

"Katy, what did you say?"

"Daddy."

John took her in his arms and hugged her like he'd never let her go again. Sarah's eyes watered but she refused to let the tears fall. Now was not the time for tears.

"Daddy," Katy rasped her voice harsh from lack of use. "The bad man is here."

"What? Where?"

"By the stable. I dropped my pie."

"Never mind about the pie. What did he look like?"

"He has a black hat, shirt and vest. He's wearing a bright red bandana around his neck."

"Sarah, you and Bertha stay here with the kids. I'm going to get the sheriff."

"Be careful," said Sarah.

"I will." He gave her a quick peck on

the lips and was off.

John, the sheriff and half a dozen men went down to the stable. The man Katy described was easy to spot. He seemed to be in charge of the other men.

The sheriff went up to the man. "Hello, Curly. I haven't seen you around these parts for a while."

"Sheriff. Been traveling."

"Enough small talk. You need to come with me. Now."

"What if I don't wanna?"

"You got no choice. My men got the drop on your men. They aren't any help to you now. There's just you, me and John Atwood, whose wife you murdered in that robbery of the Golden City Bank two years ago. He's not waiting for you to draw your gun, he's already got his out. I'm the only thing between you and a bullet. So you're gonna give me that six shooter you got on your hip. Nice and slow."

Curly looked back at his men who all had their hands up in the air. Then he looked over at John. What he saw there must have convinced him.

"What makes you so sure I'm the man you want?"

"We have a witness."

"Come on you can't believe a kid over me." Curly realized his mistake too late.

"I never said it was a kid. You're under arrest for the murder of Dorothy Atwood and five other people."

John helped the sheriff and his men take Curly and his gang to jail then returned to his family at the potluck. As soon he as walked up to them Sarah and the girls all came running.

Sarah ran her hands over him checking for wounds.

"I'm fine. No shots were fired."

"I've never been so scared in my life." She kissed him. A passionate, bedroom kind of kiss, right of front of everyone.

He wrapped his arms around her waist and kissed her back. He understood her fear. What had scared him more was that he almost shot Curly before the sheriff arrested him. He'd wanted to, for taking his wife from him, for stealing more than two years of his beautiful daughter's voice.

Finally, he and Sarah broke apart. The girls ran to them and hugged their parents. Bertha had tears in her eyes.

"Is he going to jail? Will he be punished for killing Dorothy?" asked Sarah.

"Yes, he's going to jail and will probably hang."

"Daddy what is hang?" asked Katy.

He squatted down in front of his two girls. "It means that he won't be able to hurt anyone else ever again."

"Oh."

"It's a good thing," said MaryAnn. "We don't want 'em to hurt nobody else."

"That's right," John said through tight lips. He shouldn't have to explain this to his little girls. They shouldn't have to think about people hanging. It was just another part of their childhood this man had stolen.

Sarah slipped her hand around his waist, laid her head on his chest and gave him a hug. As if she knew what he was feeling, she gave him comfort. He put his arm around her shoulder and gave it a little squeeze. He understood.

Dorothy could finally rest. Her soul at peace. Her killer caught.

"Let's go home," said Sarah.

"You young ladies ready to go home?" asked John.

"Yes, we want to get our puppies settled in their room," said MaryAnn.

"Their room?"

"Well, we thought since we share my bedroom that the puppies could have MaryAnn's room. They need some place to play. 'Course they'll sleep with us."

"Of course." John had already moved a double bed into Katy's room. She and MaryAnn refused to be parted, even at night. It was a good thing he had. Now the bed would have two puppies in it, too. Eventually, the girls would have to separate if they wanted to sleep with their dogs. If the size of the paws were any indication, these pups would be big dogs.

"You're not really going to let them sleep with the girls are you?" asked Sarah.

"Why not?"

"Fleas are why not. These dogs are going to have to be scrubbed before they come into my house."

John shrugged his shoulders. "So we'll give them a bath when we get home."

"No *we* won't. You and the girls will give them a bath. This ought to be hysterical. Bertha and I will watch from the kitchen. As long as we're going home early, I'm going to do some of my baking for tomorrow."

John put his hand on her still flat stomach and said, “Don’t you think you should rest this afternoon?”

“Why would I want to do that? I’m having a baby not becoming an invalid.” She caressed his jaw. “But thank you for caring.”

“Of course, I care.” Too much. It was becoming very easy to fall in love with his new wife. He couldn’t. Wouldn’t. It would be unfaithful to Dorothy.

CHAPTER 6

As soon as they got home the girls couldn't wait to get the puppies up to their room. They scooped up each pup and ran into the house.

"Be careful, don't run. Don't take those dogs in the house, they need baths. Girls!," Sarah called after them. They ignored her in their haste.

She closed her eyes and shook her head in exasperation. He knew how she felt, but he was still feeling grateful that this episode in his life could finally be put behind him. He had his little girl back.

Sarah went in the house with the three empty pie pans. It hadn't taken long for her pies to disappear. Now everyone knew what a gem of a cook he'd married. She was so much more than a cook. His conscience said. But there was still a part of him that loved Dorothy and was loyal to her. Dorothy was gone and Sarah was here. She wasn't going anywhere.

"You have to go get those dogs and bathe them. I'll start some water. But they need to go outside. Now."

He raised his hands in surrender. "Okay, I'm on my way."

The girls came downstairs leading their puppies by the rope the farmer gave them.

“What do you girls have to say to your Mama?” asked John.

“We’re sorry,” they said in unison.

“For…,” prompted John.

“For bringing the puppies in the house after you said not to.”

“And…,” said John.

MaryAnn and Katy hung their heads. “We’ll give them baths before we bring them back in.”

“Thank you, ladies. Now take them outside.”

The girls perked up a little bit and led the puppies outside.

“The water will be hot in a few minutes. I’ll bring it out while you get the tub.”

“Should you be carrying things, with the baby and all?”

"I'm pregnant not disabled. I'm fine. You just get the tub."

"Okay."

He got the tub and put it in the middle of the yard. Then he put in a bucket of cold water. Sarah carried out the two buckets of hot water. He put one in the tub and left the other out to rinse them with.

"MaryAnn let's do your pup first."

"We don't want this to get wet." John took the rope off and handed it to her. She handed it to Katy so she could help wash her puppy.

John picked up the dog and put it in the water. They were still small, only about six weeks old, so he couldn't get out though he yelped and tried to.

"Daddy, he doesn't like it. Let him out," cried MaryAnn.

"Not until he's clean. You want him to be able to sleep with you don't you?"

"Yes." Her little voice was so sad, John almost felt sorry for her.

"Well, he has to have a bath first. Now hand me the soap."

She handed it to him. He rubbed the soap as best he could over the squirming pup. Luckily he was still little and John could hold him in one hand and soap him with the other.

That didn't mean he didn't get wet. The pup struggled and splashed and by the time he was done with both dogs, he was as wet as they were.

He wrapped the clean, wet dog in a towel and handed it to MaryAnn.

"Now take him upstairs to your bedroom and dry him off. Don't let him down out here he'll get all muddy and we'll have to do it all over again."

"Thank you, Daddy," she said as she took the puppy in her arms.

Then he did the same thing to the other dog.

"Here you go, Katydid. Your pup is a girl so you might want to think of a girl's name for her."

She nodded and wrapped her arms around the puppy before she rushed into the house.

Sarah stood on the porch waiting for him with a towel, a dry shirt and a smile from ear to ear.

"It wasn't that funny."

"You weren't watching. It was much more fun for Bertha and me than it was for you."

“Dang dogs. Already more trouble than they’re worth,” he grumbled.

“Aw. You know they’re worth every drop of water you wore just to see the smiles on the girls faces.”

“Hrumpt,” he said as he put on the clean shirt. “We’ll see.”

Later that afternoon there were wonderful smells coming from the kitchen. He went in to see what wonders Sarah was baking. She was just getting a cookie sheet out of the oven. The table was covered in dish towels and cookies were cooling. She had six cookie sheets going. Two with cookies to go into the oven, two on the table cooling and two just coming out of the oven. She set those two on the table. Put the ones with cookies on them in the oven and took the cookies off the two that had been cooling. Then she took those to the counter and cut out more sugar cookies to bake.

"You've been busy."

She turned at the sound of his voice. "Well, hello there. You've been in your office all afternoon. I was going to bring you some coffee and cookies. Do you want some?"

"You bet. But I'll get them." He poured a cup of coffee and sat at the end of the table with the cooled cookies. "How are you feeling? You're not wearing yourself out are you?"

"I'm fine. I love to bake. It relaxes me and everyone enjoys my treats so much. It's very gratifying. I used to think of opening a bakery. But that was just a dream. Now I can make people happy this way."

"Well, never let it be said that I don't let a woman do what she loves to do. Especially when I reap the benefits." He grabbed another cookie and left to go to the barn. Just as he stepped out the kitchen door he noticed a buggy racing up the driveway. He walked to the front of the house to greet the guest.

The buggy rocked to a stop right in front of John.

"Hello, stranger, going a little fast there. I've got children and would appreciate if you wouldn't run them down in your hurry."

The man got out of the still rocking conveyance.

"I'm looking for Sarah Johnson. I was told I could find her here."

"Sarah Atwood lives here."

"That's right. She is married now, isn't she? Well, that's of little consequence to me. Would you get her?"

"Who are you and why should I get my wife?"

"I'm William Grayson, her cousin."

John looked the man over. Sarah hadn't said much about her previous life. Maybe he was what she was running from, enough to answer an advertisement for a mail order bride.

"You stay here. I'll see if she wants to see you."

John found Sarah still in the kitchen baking cookies.

"Sarah. There's someone here to see you. He says he's your cousin, William Grayson."

"William? What in the world would

he be doing here. I can't imagine him in the west. He's too…well, he's just too citified to come here."

She wiped her hands on a towel and went with John to the front. When she stepped onto the porch and saw him she was genuinely surprised.

"William? What are you doing here?" she said.

"I came to get you and bring you home." He beat his hat on his pants. Dust flew everywhere.

"Have you lost your mind? I am home. This is my home now. Not New York and never with you." Sarah stayed where she was with John next to her. She didn't go anywhere near her cousin. She had been running from him.

"Have you told him?" he sneered.

"Told him?"

"Told him about you. About MaryAnn."

John looked at Sarah. All the blood had drained from her face. She turned to him, "I…."

"So you haven't told him that you were never married. That MaryAnn is a bastard."

"William, how could you say that? You're a cruel and evil man. I'm sorry I'm related to you."

"There's no need to be upset. Of course, she told me. We don't have secrets from each other. We're married."

Anger pulsed through him. She should have told him before they married. It should have been his decision to wed her or not. Not that he would have turned her away. Once he'd seen her, he could never turn her away. But she didn't know that. He guessed that was the point. She was afraid he'd turn her away. She'd never actually said she was married, but she answered to Missus and she wore a wedding ring. What was he supposed to think?

"Now, Mr. Grayson, I suggest that you take your leave before I have to shoot you for trespassing." He touched the Colt on his hip.

"One last chance Sarah, come home with me. Come back to where you belong." He waved his hand taking in his surroundings. "Not this God forsaken place in the middle of nowhere."

"This is my home. I'm not leaving but you are. Get in that buggy and get off my property or," she grabbed John's gun from his holster and aimed it at William, "I swear I'll shoot you myself."

"You'll regret this, Sarah."

Furious, he leaped into the buggy. Standing, he took the reins in both hands and lifted them above his head. In one savage motion he brought them down upon both horses. The start was so violent Grayson would have been thrown backward all the way to the ground had the reins not stopped him. The yank on the reins, of course, brought the team to a halt.

Grayson's rage had not subsided but he did manage to regain some self control. This time he sat down and slapped the horses smartly. He drove them in a tight right turn and headed for the front gate. Taking the buggy whip from beside the seat he cracked both horses twice before even reaching the gate.

Sarah let her arms fall and her head with them. Tears ran down her face. "I'll take that now." He gently took the gun from her.

She looked up at him, tears streaked her beautiful face. "John, I'm sorry, so very sorry. I should have told you, but I was afraid…."

"You should have told me. It was my decision to make. Mine to decide if and how your background would affect me." He spat the words at her, knowing they would hurt. He wanted to hurt her, like he hurt now. She didn't trust him.

"Everything I told you was true. I never said I was married. I let you assume it, which is just as bad. Lee and I were days from being wed. But they didn't care…his superiors…they wouldn't even allow us the time to do it that day. It's the God damned army and the war that kept me from being a bride. That caused me to live in fear every time I went anywhere in New York. And Mrs. Selby knew. I didn't lie to her. She knew everything but you're right, I should have told you. And you're probably right to reject me."

"I didn't say I was rejecting you. Nor would I have rejected you had I known, but you didn't give me the chance."

"But you are. You're pushing me away, I can feel it. I'd hoped this baby would bring us closer. But I can't overcome the ghosts of the dead. Dorothy will always have your heart. And now this on top of that. I don't know if I can live like that. Live in a house where I'm not wanted."

“Sarah…”

She went inside, up to their room and slammed the door.

The smell of burning cookies came from the kitchen.

He closed his eyes. “Well, hell.”

*****

Yes, she’d been wrong to withhold the information. Yes, it should have been his decision but by his own account he wouldn’t have rejected her. So why was he now?

She’d come out of their bedroom long enough to cook and serve supper, then retreated there once again. Now it was bedtime and she expected John to come up soon, after he put the girls to bed.

She got out her nightgown and robe and put them on.

He came into the room. "The girls wondered where you were at supper. I told them you weren't feeling well."

"I guess you didn't lie to them. Anger is a form of not feeling well."

"What do you have to be angry about? I'm the one who was made a fool of." He sat on the bed and took off his boots.

"Made a fool of? What haven't I done that you asked for now or in your letters to Mrs. Selby? What aren't you getting out of this farce of a marriage? You get to bed me every night. I've given you and your employees palatable food to eat. Our daughters are best friends and doing better than either of them were before. And we have another child on the way. So what aren't you getting?"

"I'm not getting a wife I can trust."

He stood, took off his shirt.

"And that's what's between us, keeping you from loving me? A lack of trust? Well, I wish I could trust you, with my heart, but you'd just stomp on it like you do to everyone who tries to get close to you. Maybe Katy would've talked if you'd spent some time with her."

"That's enough," he yelled. "Leave Katy out of this."

She took a deep breath. "You're right. I'm sorry. This is about you and me, not our girls."

"Yes, it is." He reached for his belt and undid it, dropping his pants to the floor.

"You might as well leave those on. If you think we're having sex tonight, you're dead wrong."

"Why? Because you're angry?"

"Yes. Dammit. I don't want you anywhere near me. I'm leaving."

"And going where?"

"I'll sleep in MaryAnn's room. She and Katy share Katy's room as it is."

"That's the puppies' room."

She stared at him. Couldn't believe what he'd just said. "Did you just tell me I couldn't sleep in another room because it belonged to the puppies?"

"Yes."

She laughed. Try as she might, she couldn't help it. It was so stupid. This whole situation was stupid.

When she looked up at John, he had a smile on his face, too.

"What are we going to do about this? Neither one of us was very open or very trusting. You about Dorothy and me about…well me. If you can't love me, why should I stay? Tell me, John. Why?"

"For our girls."

She bit back the tears. "For our girls."

"And the baby that you carry."

"Can you tell me that we should really be bringing a baby into this mess? That we should subject another person to our mock marriage."

He sat down on the bed and scrubbed his face with his hands. "There has to be a way. Come to bed."

"No." She tied her robe. "I'm sleeping in the doghouse, where I belong." She took one of the lamps, walked quietly out of the room and down the hall to MaryAnn's bedroom. The room was empty, as she suspected it would be. The pups were sleeping with their little mistresses. She tiptoed across the hall and opened the door to the girl's bedroom. Sure enough there were both little girls and the two dogs sleeping soundly. One of the pups raised its head but went back to sleep when he saw she presented no threat.

Sarah smiled, closed the door and went back across the hall and crawled into the bed.

*****

She woke to strong arms picking her up out of bed. "What? What are you doing?" she asked as she automatically put her arms around his neck. "John, what are you doing?"

"We may be many things to each other and we may be angry with each other, but you are my wife and you will sleep in my bed. No one is going to suspect we aren't the happily married couple that we were earlier today." He carried her back to their room and dropped her on the bed. He had his drawers on so at least he wasn't running around the house naked.

"I'm not going to make love to you," she said.

"I'm not asking you to." He got into bed and pulled her into his side.

She didn't stop him. Didn't ask what the heck he thought he was doing. She understood. He was used to her. Used to her sleeping with him. He couldn't sleep without her.

It was a start.

CHAPTER 7

It was a brutal, bloody trek back to Golden City. Upon arrival at the stables the owner of the team threatened to shoot Grayson when he saw the condition of the horses.

"I will never rent you another animal and if I even see you get near a horse you will be the one tasting this whip!"

Grayson soothed his rage with a five dollar gold piece and then went straight to the Chicago Saloon and a glass of the rot gut they called whiskey.

After his third whiskey a plan began to emerge. He would have Sarah or no one would. He called the barkeep over.

"Where would I go to find men to do a job for me?"

"What kind of job?"

"One they won't ask questions about."

"Go to Spurs. Two streets north, in the alley on the right side of the street. Tell the bartender, Joe sent you."

"Thank you, my good man." He gave Joe a dollar for his trouble and his silence. Then he headed out the door to Spurs."

Spurs was as disreputable a place as William had ever been in. No one looked up when he entered. Preferring instead to keep their heads down and concentrate on their drinks. There were no girls and no music. This was a place for drinking. Period.

The barkeep came over. “What’s yer poison?”

“Whiskey. Joe sent me.”

Two of the men at a nearby table perked up and looked his way.

“What ya lookin’ fer?”

“I have a job I need done. No questions asked.”

“What’s it pay?” asked the barkeep.

“Fifty dollars now and another fifty when it’s done.”

“Well now, me and Bobby Ray can do just about any job you got,” said one of the men from the table.

“Is there some place we can talk?”

“Sure. Clancy we need the backroom,” the man called to the barkeep.

"You know where it is."

"Come with me, Mister…."

"Smith. William Smith."

"Well, Mr. Smith, come with us. I'm sure we can do business."

*****

The more Sarah thought about it, the more she liked the idea. John had stopped making love to her. The only time they touched was when they slept. John still insisted on holding her while they slept. They barely talked except at meals when it was needed to keep up appearances. She was sure that Bertha knew things were strained between them even if the cowboys didn't. Bertha was with Sarah every day.

"When are you two going to make up?"

"I don't know what you're talking

about."

"I'm talking about the fact that the tension around here is thick enough to cut with a knife. About the fact that the only time either of you smile is with the girls and then only when the other one of you isn't around."

"It's going to be fine Bertha. We're just going through a rough patch."

"Well, I hope you get through it soon. This past week has been hell. Everyone is walking on eggshells around you. Even the girls feel it."

"Oh, Bertha, tell me you're exaggerating about the girls. We've been trying to keep them away from this."

"Well, yer doin' a piss poor job of it."

"Oh, God. I'll talk to John. The girls are more important than anything."

"I should hope so."

"Your point is made."

"Hrumpt."

That night Sarah put the girls to bed and then put on her robe. She'd been wearing a nightgown since the fight. A reminder that they were no longer intimate. Tonight she wore only the robe. She was going to fight fire with fire.

She waited up for John. He'd been making it a habit to work in his office until he was sure she was asleep. Tonight would be different.

John came into the bedroom after midnight. Sarah was sitting up in the middle of the bed with her robe open to the waist. He stopped in the middle of the room.

"What are you doing up?"

"I wanted to talk to you."

“Put on some clothes.”

“Fine.” She shoved the robe off one of her shoulders and looked up at him. His eyes smoldered. She did the other shoulder. The robe now pooled at her elbows and her breasts were exposed.

“Cover up or I won’t be responsible.”

In answer she released her arms from the robe.

He was on her in two strides, pulling her up from the bed until she stood in his arms

“I warned you.”

His mouth crashed down on hers. She wrapped her arms around his neck and grasped the back of his head keeping him at her lips.

She backed off, gasping for air. “So you did.”

"Did what?"

"Warn me."

"I did."

She began unbuttoning his shirt. "When are you going to forgive me?"

"I already have."

"Then why have you stayed angry?"

"I'm angry at myself for the way I treated you. I was no different than the people in New York. I was ashamed."

She ran her hands up and down his chest. "I understand and I should have told you. I should never have assumed that Mrs. Selby would have told you. I'm so sorry John. I'm sorry that you found out the way you did."

"No, I'm sorry. I should…."

She placed her fingers on his lips.

"Shhh. It doesn't matter. Just make

love to me. I've missed you."

In answer he picked her up and placed her gently on the bed. Then he rid himself of his remaining clothes and came down next to her.

He tried to be gentle with her. She knew he did but she would have none of it. She rolled him to his back and impaled herself on his hard length.

"Sarah!"

"I don't want gentle. I've waited too long. I want you now." And she began to ride him.

He kept up with the rhythm she set, following her stroke for stroke. Then he reached down and touched her and she exploded, shattered. He followed her with his own climax. Waves of pleasure rolled off her and she collapsed onto his chest.

Spent.

John wrapped his arms around her and turned them so they were on their sides. He didn't leave her and she was glad. She liked for him to fill her. It was at times like this that she really felt they were two halves of one person. It was the only time she truly felt whole.

"John?"

His eyes were closed.

"Don't fall asleep on me yet."

"Alright." He opened his brown eyes and she watched them darken in anticipation of round two. "What do you need?"

"We've been affecting everyone, including the girls. We can't do that. When we fight we have to keep it to this room."

"Agreed. I don't like to fight with you."

"Nor I you. We have to make a promise to communicate better with each other."

"I promise I will try to understand you. To see things from your perspective if you will try to see them from mine."

"I promise to do the same. And I promise to spell out everything and not assume you can read my mind."

"Me, too."

"All that being said, do you have any questions for me?"

"Yes. What was your life like before you came here?

"We had a good life thanks to Aunt Gertrude. My parents threw me out as soon as they found out I was pregnant. I went to Aunt Gertrude, my great aunt actually. She was my father's aunt though she was only two years older than he was. One look at me in my pitiful state on her door step and she let me in and I stayed. She helped me raise MaryAnn. That's why she's such a little adult instead of a child. I don't think she's ever had anyone to play with. Oh, Aunt Gertrude and I did our best but it wasn't enough."

"She has Katy now. Mrs. Selby was right about that. They are the best of friends."

"Yes, she was right wasn't she?"

"I don't like fighting with you, but I sure like the making up part."

She smiled at him. "Me, too."

"We didn't hurt the baby did we?"

"No. The baby is just fine."

He cuddled her closer. "Good."

"John, I'd like to talk about

something. I did some thinking while we weren't speaking and when I thought you were going to throw me out."

"I never, never will throw you out."

"I'm glad. I don't want to go anywhere. I was going to open a bakery in Golden City if you did. I have that money that Aunt Gertrude left me and I'd already figured that MaryAnn and I could live above the bakery. MaryAnn and Katy would still be able to see each other that way. I wouldn't take the girls away from each other if I can help it."

He'd been caressing her hip and thigh, rubbing up and down while she spoke. "You don't need to open a bakery or go anywhere. I don't want you to leave and will never throw you out. No matter how mad we get at each other, we are married for life. I take my vow seriously."

His hand moved to her back and he rubbed it starting in small circles and getting larger.

"I do, too. But it is important to me to know that I can take care of MaryAnn and me if I need to."

He nodded and kissed her chin. "I can understand, coming from your background, that you would need that sense of security. I'll do whatever I need to in order for you to feel secure."

"Thank you." She caressed his face. "We should sleep now."

"Yes, we should."

She felt him stir against her.

"We can sleep later." She said, rolling them until she was on her back. "Much later."

*****

Sarah made biscuits. Rolled out the dough, cut it and hummed all the while.

"Well, someone is happier today," said Bertha.

"Yes. You don't have to worry anymore. We had a good long talk last night."

"Good. The girls will be glad to hear it."

"We'll talk to them this morning."

"As you should. What do you want me to do first this morning? Chickens or cows?"

"Gather the eggs, please and then milk the cows. I'll finish these and get some pancake batter started."

Bertha left to do her morning chores and Sarah started her batter. When Bertha returned with the eggs and milk for the day, Sarah kept the eggs she'd need for her baking and scrambled the rest with bits of sausage in them. Today they'd make butter. They were down to their last bowl and she needed that for the pancakes. She'd made some syrup from a jar of the blueberries she'd found down in the cellar, to serve with them.

Finally, all the food was ready and she beat the triangle to call the men. Sarah had almost all the food on the table by the time everyone was seated at it and eating. She saw that they needed more biscuits and got up to get them. When she picked them up off the counter, she glanced out the window above the sink and saw smoke.

"Smoke! It looks like the barn is on fire."

"Let's go men. Sarah, you and Bertha stay here with the girls. I'm sure it'll be fine but I don't want to have to worry about you."

"We'll be fine. Just go stop that before it spreads." She gave him a quick kiss. "Be safe."

He caressed her cheek. "I will."

He ran out the door to join the other men and fight the fire. Sarah sent Bertha with the girls upstairs and she began to put the food away to stay warm so the men could eat when they were done or when they got a break.

"Well, isn't this just the picture of domesticity?"

Sara swung around. "William. What are you doing here? I thought I told you to leave."

"You did but you don't seem to understand. I can't leave until you go with me."

"Are you crazy? I'm not going with you. My home is here. With John and the girls."

"Girls? You have another one besides MaryAnn? Well good for MaryAnn. It's better if she doesn't come anyway, being a bastard and all. We can start over."

Sarah backed up to the sink and reached behind her until she touched the knife she'd used on the sausage that morning. She gripped it and brought it around and brandished it in front of her. "You started the fire didn't you? You get out of here, William, before you and I both do something we'll regret."

He laughed. "Do you expect me to be

afraid of a kitchen knife? Don't be silly my dear. I came prepared." He pulled a derringer from his pocket and pointed it at her.

The knife clattered to the floor.

"Wise choice. Actually, I didn't start the fire. Some of my associates did. I can tell I may have some problems with you understanding that you have *no* choice here. You are coming with me. I'm going to take you back to New York. We're going to marry and be happy. Do you understand?"

Sarah didn't answer, unable to comprehend what he was telling her.

"Answer me, Sarah. Or I'll have to go get MaryAnn and have her come with us so that I'll have someone to hurt if you don't cooperate."

"You wouldn't. Even you can't be

that evil."

He laughed again. "I thought you just called me crazy. If that's the case, you shouldn't be surprised by anything that I do."

"Why William? You know that I'll never love you, that as of now I loathe you."

"You are all I've ever wanted. Since the first time I laid eyes on you I wanted you. I was sure that when Mother died you would turn to me. Instead, you sign up to be a mail order bride, of all things. That was a move I didn't anticipate."

"It was either that or prostitution. Even prostitution is preferable to you."

"You are not going to anger me. I know that's what you want. You want to make me angry, hoping I'll make a mistake, but I won't. Now come with me Sarah. If you don't, I will hurt MaryAnn. I don't want to but you will give me no choice."

Sarah moved toward him knowing that for now she was out of choices. He moved to the side of the door and let her go before him.

"I've parked the buggy on the other side of that small shed with the chickens in it."

"It's called a chicken coop. You brought a buggy?" She shook her head. "You didn't bring just a horse but a buggy. Don't you realize that John will come after you?"

"Why? He can just get another woman the way he got you. Mail for one." He laughed as his cruel remark.

"I don't know how many ways I can say it, you're insane William, totally insane."

They walked slowly to the chicken coop. Sarah still had hope that John would come.

"What makes you think this man will come after you? Surely, you don't think he's fallen in love with you. After such a short time? No, don't be ridiculous. Ah, I understand now. You've fallen in love with him, haven't you?"

"Don't be absurd."

"But you have. You can't even look at me and deny it."

"So what if I have? I'm allowed some happiness. I've been punished for long enough."

"You will never be punished enough. To let them lie with you…first that Lee, MaryAnn's father, and now this man. You would never let me. As much as I loved you and was kind to you, you never even thought about me, did you?"

Sarah walked slowly, as slow as she could without seeming to. If John or someone saw the buggy or saw him come into the house, then she might have a chance. Otherwise, she was going to have to go with him until they caught up but how long would that be and would John come after her at all?

The small voice inside of her that kept her down, said he wouldn't come. He didn't love her, he'd be well rid of her. But what of MaryAnn? John would keep her. She was good for Katy and he loved her. At least if she died, she knew MaryAnn would be safe.

The other voice in her said she was

strong and wanted. She wasn't the downtrodden woman that left New York. She had friends here and John may not love her yet, but he cared and he accepted her.

She stopped.

"What are you doing? Keep walking. The buggy is just around the corner."

"No."

"What do you mean no? You know what I'll do? I will do it." He started to turn away.

"No you won't. I won't let you hurt my family."

"You bitch. All this trouble I've gone through for you and you decide now is the time to discover your backbone."

"If you're smart, William, you'll take that buggy and leave. If John finds you before you get back to New York, you're a dead man."

She turned and saw John running toward her. William saw him too. He raised his gun to fire. Sarah didn't think. She just moved in front of the bullet meant for the man she loved. It struck her in the left shoulder and she fell to the ground.

William looked at her with horror in his eyes. He turned, ran around the corner of the chicken coop to the buggy and took off. Then John was there beside her.

"Sarah, honey, are you all right? Sarah. Sarah."

Strong arms picked her up and cuddled her against his broad chest. John. He'd come for her. She tried to speak. Everything was so hard and she hurt, God, she hurt. Why did it hurt so much?

"John, I didn't let him take me. I

didn't go with him."

"No you didn't. I'm proud of you, Sarah. Sarah."

Her head fell back. She was unconscious. That may be just as well. The bullet wound looked bad.

Bertha came running. "How is she?"

"Send one of the men for the doctor. If he's not at his office, find him."

John carried her inside and up the stairs to their room.

"Bertha, get some towels and put water on to boil. I've got to look at the wound and clean it."

"You got it boss." She hurried away.

"Sarah, I don't know if you can hear me or not, but I'm not going to let you go. Not now, not ever. I can't lose you, too. I love you. Can you hear me? Sarah, I love you."

She didn't move.

John took his knife and cut her blouse off and then her chemise. He checked for a wound on her back and didn't find one. The bullet was still in her.

Bertha came in with the towels. He got the pitcher and basin from on top of the commode. The water wasn't hot but was better than nothing. He had to see the wound. After dipping one of the towels in the water, he wiped the blood away, cleaning it as best he could. The blood was slowing, which was a good thing; at least she wasn't going to bleed to death.

He didn't know how deep the bullet went; just that it was still in there and needed to come out. The doc better get there soon.

Bertha helped him get her out of the rest of her clothes. He put her under the covers and tried to keep her warm, waiting for the doctor. It had been about an hour since he'd sent the man for the doctor and they still weren't back. The sound of hooves pounding hard up the drive took him to the window. His man was back but the doctor wasn't with him.

The thunder of boots on the stairs stopped when his man, Ben, pushed open the door. "Boss, the doc wasn't in. He's up the canyon helpin' with a birthin'. I left a message with his missus to send him out here as soon as he got back."

There was no choice now.

"Bertha, bring hot water, whiskey and laudanum. We've got to get the bullet out of there."

"Sure thing." She bustled out of the room and down to the kitchen.

Ben stood in the room and stared at Sarah.

"You go on and keep watch for the doctor."

"Ah. Sure. Sure." He left the room.

John was alone with Sarah. "Honey, this is going to hurt. But I'm going do the best I can to hurry and get that out of you so you'll get well."

"Daddy?"

Oh, Christ, the girls. He'd been so worried about Sarah, he'd completely forgotten the little ones.

He went over to them where they stood in the doorway. "Katy. You and MaryAnn go to your room and stay there with the puppies. Can you do that for me?"

"But Mama," said MaryAnn.

"Mama, is going to be fine. You just do as I ask."

"Yes, sir," they said together.

He saw the look in their eyes, worry and fear. Katy wouldn't lose another mother. He would not let it happen. He gave them both a hug and sent them on their way.

"Sarah, you hear that? Our girls are worried about you. You have to get well now."

Bertha came back in to the room carrying a teakettle full of boiling water. He threw the bloody water in the basin out the window, filled it with the water from the kettle and put his knife in to soak. He pulled Sarah's tweezers from off the top of the tall boy dresser and dropped them in, too.

"Here, thought you'd need these too and I didn't want to make another trip." She handed him the hemostats.

He added those to the basin. After they had soaked for a bit he took them out and put them on a towel. Then he used the water in the basin to wash his hands and then held the instruments over the basin and poured whiskey over them. That was as sterile as he could make them.

Taking the knife he made one inch incisions on the upper and lower side of the hole from the bullet. He put the knife aside and took a deep breath before he plunged his finger in the wound, working it down until he ran into the bullet. It wasn't too deep and he felt confident he could get it out with the hemostats. He wiped his hand dry, picked up the instrument and put it into the wound until he hit the lead. Then he carefully grabbed it and pulled it out. He dropped the whole thing into the basin with a splash. Then he took the whiskey and poured it into the wound.

Sarah screamed. Even unconscious she'd felt the pain. Bertha mixed some laudanum in a glass of water and fed it to Sarah. It would help keep her asleep at least while he sewed up the wound.

He hated this. His stomach roiled and threatened to bolt because it was Sarah. Seeing her like this scared the crap out of him. He could lose her, like he lost Dorothy. That wasn't going to happen. He was here this time.

After he sewed her up he cleaned her again and brought the sheets up under her arms. Now, he needed to go see his girls but first he washed the blood off his hands. No sense scaring them more than they already were.

He opened the door to Katy's room. Both girls were on the bed, the puppies under it nipping at their toes. It was one of their favorite games.

MaryAnn saw him in the doorway and came running.

"We did like you said and stayed in here until you came to get us. How's Mama?"

He picked her up in his arms. "Your Mama was hurt this morning, but she's going to be fine. I'll take you in to see her as soon as she wakes up, okay?"

MaryAnn nodded, tears in her eyes, then wrapped her arms around his neck and laid her head on his shoulder.

Katy came over and hugged his pant leg. He picked her up too and walked to the bed where he sat down and held his daughters. They both cried softly for a little while and then cuddled into him. Soft sniffles coming from both girls.

"Okay, now. I'm going to go check on Mama. I want you to go with Bertha to the kitchen and get something to eat. Are you hungry?"

Both girls shook their heads, no.

"Well you need to eat something anyway. Mama would want you to keep up your strength. Isn't that right?"

They both nodded.

He kissed each girl on top of the head. "Now go on and tell Bertha I said you could each have two cookies."

His daughters scrambled off his lap at

the thought of an extra treat.

MaryAnn stopped at the door and turned back. “You sure she’ll be okay?”

“Yes, sweet. I’ll take care of her and she’ll be right as rain.”

“I guess that’s alright then. She trusts you and so do I.”

He was touched. Sarah and MaryAnn trusted him. Considering their background, that was their world they were laying at his feet. He could lift it up or crush it. They trusted him to do what was right.

Across the hall, Sarah was trying to wake up. She thrashed in the bed until he sat with her and held her. He really didn’t know what he would do if he lost her. He wasn’t equipped to raise one girl much less two on his own. Sure, he had Bertha, but it wasn’t the same as having a mother and he had no intention of marrying again.

Sarah stirred and opened her eyes. They got large and she said, "William. He's insane. He thinks I'm going to leave with him. Leave everything and everyone I love to go with him. No, I won't. I'd rather die."

"Hush now. You're not going to die." I need you, he added silently.

"He shot me. I remember he was going to shoot you with that little gun."

He sat on the bed next to her. "It never would have reached me. He had a derringer and must not have known much about it. Promise me you will never do that again. You're giving me gray hair. And scaring the girls who are afraid their mother is going to die like Dorothy did."

"Oh, the girls. Are they alright? William threatened to hurt MaryAnn if I didn't go with him."

John growled and said under his breath, "that's another reason for me to kill him."

"What?"

"Nothing. She's fine and you shouldn't get worked up. See. You've started bleeding again." He got a clean towel and blotted the blood away.

"William? What happened to him?"

"He got away."

"You've got to tell the sheriff. He's the one who started the fire. Well actually, he hired some men to do it. He wanted everyone out of the house. John, he'll try again. He's absolutely insane."

"I'll talk to the sheriff. Now I want you to drink this and try to rest."

"What is it?"

"A little laudanum in water. Just enough to relax you so you can get some rest."

He helped her sit up so she could drink the water. "Alright. Where's the doctor? I want to thank him."

"You're looking at him."

"You did this?"

"I tried to wait for the doctor, but he was up the canyon helping with a birth. No telling when he'll get here, so I took the bullet out and sewed you up."

"Thank you, John." She yawned. "I seem to be getting sleepy."

"Good. Just lay back and I'll cover you up so you can sleep."

His words fell on deaf ears. She was already asleep. Now he'd watch her. He knew enough from watching Dorothy care for one of their drovers, who'd gotten trampled. The first twenty-four hours were the worst. It would be bad if she developed a fever. For now he held her hand and watched her sleep.

CHAPTER 8

Sarah ran as fast as her legs would carry her but William was catching up. Faster, she must go faster. There was a hitch in her side but she ignored it. He would kill her and MaryAnn. She must get to MaryAnn. Protect MaryAnn.

Then she remembered. John had MaryAnn, she was safe. John would protect her. John. He would protect them all.

William was upon her. He held her by the neck and tried to kiss her. She turned her head back and forth, evading him. Kicking him, she screamed until the band around her neck tightened and she couldn't breathe any longer.

His face was on her. She screamed and screamed.

John found her. She was safe. She breathed in his fresh scent and relaxed into his arms.

John held her. She thrashed around and screamed in pain. Her eyes opened and then she stopped and was still. Breathing easier, her eyes closed. He checked her forehead and she was hot. Fever was upon her along with her nightmares.

He dipped a towel into the clean water in the basin, wrung it out and put it on her forehead. At first she shied away from it and then she pressed into it, wanted the cool, the relief from the heat it provided.

She continued to burn with fever. John rubbed her down with a cool cloth. He stroked it over her arms, neck and chest. Then he did her face. Each time was the same, she moaned softly and leaned into the cloth.

The doctor finally arrived early the next morning.

"I came as soon as I could. Did you take the lead out?"

John nodded. "Yes. It didn't appear to have nicked anything vital and the bullet came out whole. I don't know what's causing the fever."

"It could be anything. I doubt it's something you did or didn't do. You did all the things I would have, so stop beating yourself up about it."

"But she's so fragile."

"Sarah will be fine. Just get as much liquid down her as possible and try to keep her cool. When the fever breaks she'll probably get the chills. They you'll have to keep her warm.

"Okay, doc. I'll keep an eye on her."

The doctor put his stethoscope back in his bag. "Don't forget to take care of yourself. You have two little girls that are scared and need you, too."

"Don't worry, Doc. Between me and Bertha we'll make it."

John didn't show the doctor out. He wanted, no needed, to stay by Sarah's side.

"Come on, sweetheart. Come back to us, to me. I can't lose you Sarah."

Bertha came in with more water and some beef broth. "I'm not the best cook but

I don't figure she'll mind none."

"Thank you, Bertha."

"Think nothing of it. Now I've got supper on the table. You need to go down and be with your daughters for a while. They're real scared, boss. They need to see their daddy. Need to know everything is going to be alright."

"I know. Thanks for staying with her."

"I love her too, boss."

He nodded to her and walked out of the room.

Love? He'd told her he loved her but did he? He was scared, scared she might die and leave him. Was that love? He knew he loved MaryAnn. He recognized it because it was like his love for Katy. But he'd never felt like this about any woman. He thought he'd loved Dorothy and she him. But in reality they were comfortable with each other, not in love. He'd never felt the overwhelming need to be with her or fear that he couldn't be, like he did with Sarah.

Losing Sarah would be like losing a part of himself. The best part.

He stopped in the kitchen doorway and watched the people at the table. Ten grown men and two little girls. All quiet and all barely eating. He didn't think it was Bertha's cooking that kept them from eating or kept the conversation to a whisper.

He plastered a smile on his face. "What are you all so quiet for? Sarah's going to be just fine, but if she wakes up and finds this place turned into a funeral parlor in her absence she's going to be pi…," he stopped, looked at his daughters and modified his words, "upset."

"Is Mama really going to be okay?" MaryAnn asked, tears welling in her eyes.

"Yes, she really is but it's going to take a while and until then I need you and Katy to be real strong for her. Can you do that?"

MaryAnn leaned over and whispered in Katy's ear. Katy nodded and looked at her father.

"Katy and I will be good and help Bertha. We can pick up our rooms and dust and milk the cows, and…and" she burst into tears and Katy followed.

"Come here both of you." The girls climbed up into his lap, one on each leg. He hugged them to him and held them close until their crying subsided.

"Now listen to me. I know you're

scared. I'm scared too, but the best thing we can do is just let Mama rest and try to keep our spirits high for her."

"Daddy, why did Uncle William shoot Mama? I don't understand."

William. Just the sound of his name on her innocent lips was enough to send him into a rage, but he held it back for the girls.

"He's a very sick man and didn't mean to shoot your Mama. He was aiming for me and your Mama jumped in the way. She was trying to save my life."

"Why'd he wanna kill you?"

"Well, he thought if I was gone that your Mama would want to go with him back to New York to live."

"Away from here? Away from Katy?"

Though Katy talked now, she was still

letting MaryAnn do all of their talking and she just shook her head. Then both girls started to cry again.

"Hush now. That's not going to happen. We are a family and your Mama is going to get better. You'll see. It's going to be fine." He hoped he was telling them the truth. Only time would tell.

Sarah burned with fever for three days waking for only short periods. John made her drink water and broth during those times she was awake. He gave her laudanum only when she appeared to be in pain. The last thing he needed was to get her hooked on the stuff. He nursed her alone refusing to let Bertha help except during supper which he took with the girls. They seemed to like knowing that Daddy was taking care of Mama and he reassured them every day that

Mama was going to be okay.

On the third day the fever broke and Sarah woke up. She was drenched and he got her out of her nightgown and into a fresh one while Bertha put fresh dry linens on the bed. Doc was right. It didn't take her long to get the chills. John put extra blankets on the bed and when that didn't help he stripped them both, got in bed with her and held her close.

She shivered violently and he wrapped one of his legs over hers to help stop the tremors.

"I'm so cold."

"I know love, but it will pass. The worst is past."

"I hope you're right about that."

Suddenly she turned in his arms. "John, the baby…?"

"Is fine," he soothed her, running his hands up and down her back. "He's just fine."

She settled a bit then. "I was so scared for you. I didn't know that he couldn't have hit you with the bullet."

He held her closer. "I know. Did I thank you for saving me?"

"No. You just scolded me for doing it."

"Well," he tucked her hair behind her ear. "Thank you. You didn't know and I could be wrong about the distance his derringer could shoot. They're making them accurate at greater distances now. Considering that he probably bought the best that money could buy, you probably did save my life. But that doesn't mean I ever want you to do that again. You've scared the hell out of me these last days."

"Does that mean you want me to stay?"

"Hell, yes. Do you have any idea what my life would be like without you? We'd have to eat Bertha's cooking." He teased her, just so happy that she was going to be alright.

"I knew it. You only want me for my cooking." She lay back in his arms, just the little bit of teasing taking all her energy.

"You know that's not true." He kissed her forehead thankful to find it cool. "I want you for lots of things."

She gave a small shiver and cuddled closer and sleepily said. "I love you, John. Thank you for keeping me." Then she was sound asleep. The chills had subsided enough for her to rest.

"I love you, too," he said to her sleeping form. John held her in his arms. Almost afraid to let her go, that he might lose her. Had it really taken this close call for him to realize he loved her? He hadn't wanted to love her, he knew now that he used being unfaithful to Dorothy as an excuse. A way to keep her at bay, but his heart had seen through to what his brain refused to grasp. He'd never really loved Dorothy, not really. Not like he loved Sarah. She'd come into his heart with that first blush and entrenched herself there after their first kiss. A kiss so sweet he still remembered it like it was yesterday, not months ago.

And Katy loved her, too. She and MaryAnn were sisters, not to be parted. Yes, they were afraid they'd lose their mother but they were just as afraid they'd lose each other. He couldn't let that happen.

Sarah loved him. She'd told him so. She may have been gripped in the aftermath of a fever when she said it but that was all the more reason it was true.

He rested his cheek against the top of her head and fell asleep. After keeping vigil in the rocker while she burned with fever, this was the first time in days he'd really slept. With her safe in his arms.

*****

Sarah woke to John suckling her nipples.

"There you are. I was wondering how long I'd get to play before you woke up." He grinned at her, his dimples creasing his cheeks the way she loved.

"You are a bad man, waking me like

that," but she ran her fingers through his thick brown hair and brought his lips up to hers for a kiss.

"I think you like it and I think that's the way I'll wake you from now on." He lifted himself away from her. "Do you feel like going downstairs for breakfast today? If you don't I'll have the girls come in here. They're anxious to see you."

"I'll go down if you'll help me. I feel pretty weak." She buttoned up her nightgown.

"Of course. Let's get your robe on you. I'm bringing you right back here after you eat and everyone gets to fawn over you for awhile."

"You're just ready for them to know that I'll be cooking again soon."

While he looked for her robe he said,

"Not true. We've actually had some good meals from Bertha. She does breakfast really well now. I think she learned something while helping you. We've even had breakfast for supper, which was a blessing since her suppers still leave something to be desired."

He found her robe and helped her into it over her nightgown, then picked her up in his arms.

"John!" she wrapped her arms around his neck. "What are you doing?"

"I'm carrying you down to breakfast. I don't want you falling and you admitted you're still very weak from you're ordeal."

She laid her head on his shoulder. "Alright. I'll let you, if you don't think I'm too heavy."

He groaned dramatically. "I think I'll

manage."

Sarah laughed. "What has you in such a good mood this morning?"

"You. You're better and are going to be right as rain with a little rest. We've got two beautiful daughters and are going to have another one or a son in a few months. What could I not be happy about?"

He carried her into the kitchen and the cowhands burst into applause when they saw her and the girls ran over and hugged her legs as that was all they could reach.

John sat at the head of the table with her in his lap. She hugged each of the girls and assured them she was all right. She could have insisted that he put her in her own chair but she kind of liked it just where she was. The girls sat on either side of her. Bertha was so happy to have her back she piled a plate high with all kinds of food.

"Bertha, thank you, but I really only want some toasted bread and coffee. I don't think my stomach can handle much else."

"Of course not," said Bertha. "I don't know what I was thinking. Boss, that can be your plate. I'll fix the missus what she wants." She bustled away to get the coffee.

Sarah drank about half the coffee and ate one piece of bread. She turned to John and said quietly, "I think I'm ready to go back upstairs."

He stood and announced, "I'm taking her upstairs now so she can rest. If she's still feeling better you'll see her again at supper." Everyone said goodbye and John carried her back to their room.

"John, I need a bath."

He wrinkled his nose. "I believe

you're right."

She punched him in the shoulder.

He put her down on the bed so she could sit up. "I'll have Bertha start some water boiling. You wait here while I go get the tub. Don't do anything until I get back."

She nodded and said, "Go. The sooner you're gone the sooner I get my bath."

He walked out of the room and she immediately stood up only to fall back to the bed. It was going to be really hard to use the chamber pot this way. It was behind the screen and the screen was clear on the other side of the room. She eased her way down the length of the bed to the foot post. Using that as a brace she stood and though wobbly, her legs held her. She leaned into the post and waited a bit letting her legs get used to her weight again. That was how he found her.

"What the hell are you doing?"

The long metal tub clattered to the floor.

"I'm going to use the chamber pot."

"I'll help you."

"This is so embarrassing."

"Who do you think helped you while you were sick? I can help you now."

Having no choice she let him support her.

He helped her back to the bed and sat her down on it.

"Now, are you going to stay put this time? Or do I have to hog tie you?"

"You can get the water for my bath. I'll be good."

He looked at her and raised an

eyebrow. "You promise?"

"Yes, I promise." She crossed her heart. "I'm not going to say 'and hope to die' because I came too close to that."

He just nodded but she saw something like anguish cross his face and then it was gone. "But you didn't and you're here. To stay."

When he came back with the water, one bucket of each hot and cold, she was still sitting where he'd left her.

"Ah, good girl, to wait for her husband to help her."

"I didn't want to get scolded again. Are you going to help me out of these clothes now? That water looks inviting."

He poured the buckets of water into the tub and then closed the door before coming to her.

"Okay, let's get you out of those clothes."

She undid her robe and shrugged out of it. He undid all the buttons on her gown and then had her stand, using him for support, while he pulled it down her arms and over her hips. Then he picked her up and set her in the tub.

The water was wonderful, hot and relaxing. "We're going to need more water if I'm going to wash my hair."

"You sit in there and soak and I'll get some more water."

She raised her knees and scooted down until she could lie back in the bottom of the tub. Sarah just lay there, letting the hot water soak into her sore muscles. Who would have thought that being sick would leave her so tired. She tried to reach up with both of her arms and that's when her bullet wound decided to make her remember it was there. Putting her arm back down, she used the right arm to cover her hair with water.

When John returned with the water, he nearly dropped the buckets because he couldn't see anything but her knees sticking up from the tub. He set the buckets down and came to the side of the tub and stared down at her.

"What are you doing?"

"Wetting my hair. I was going to wash it but I can't lift my left arm high enough."

"Here, let's get you sitting up and I'll wash your hair." He put his hands under her arms and lifted her like she weighed no more than one of the girls. He took the soap and ran it over her head working up a lather which he worked down her back to the ends. Then he helped her lie back in the water and rinse her hair.

He helped her back up and washed her body for her, taking extra time around her breasts and between her legs. She leaned back against his chest and enjoyed the ministrations.

"I can't make love to you. You're much too weak and sore, but I want to," he said as he removed his hands and got a bucket of now warm water.

"You're right. I think an orgasm now would kill me."

He chuckled. "Sit up and let me rinse your hair."

She did and he poured warm water over her.

"That feels so good. Now comes the

hard part. You have to detangle and comb my hair."

"Nothing to it. You've seen Katy's hair after her bath and I did hers for a lot of years. I think I can do yours."

"Good because I can't with my arm."

He had her sit up on the bed and put her nightgown on. Then he sat next to her and combed her hair working from the bottom up. Once he had all the tangles out of it he gave it one last comb through and then braided it in a single plait down her back, just like she'd worn it when he taught her to ride.

"There. Do you feel better?"

"Much."

He covered her with the blankets and then stretched out next to her and took her in his arms.

"I'm glad your back."

"So am I. We have to talk about what happened," said Sarah.

"What happened is William tried to take you and then, when he couldn't, he tried to kill me and force you to go with him."

"I guess that about sums it up. Except what do we do now? I don't think he's going to give up. Not now. He's still going to try to kill you and may try to hurt MaryAnn. If he finds out I survived, he'll be back for me, too."

"We'll just have to make sure that doesn't happen."

"You almost make me think you care."

"Of course, I care. I almost lost you. I've never been so scared in my life." He squeezed her closer and her shoulder felt the pain.

"Owww. Not so tight."

He immediate relaxed his hold. "Sorry, I forgot your shoulder.

"No, I'm sorry. I shouldn't have said what I did. I know you took care of me while I was sick. You didn't have to. You could have had Bertha do it. Our relationship has been rocky and I'm feeling vulnerable, that's all."

He lifted her chin with his knuckle until she looked at him. "I'm not going to lose you. Not to William and not to my own stupidity. We are a family, you, me, the girls and this baby. Nothing and no one is going to change that. Are we clear?"

However harsh he sounded, she heard the love behind the words. He loved her.

She knew it. She wondered if he did. She cuddled a little closer. “Yes. We’re clear.”

“Good.” He shifted so his lips claimed hers in the sweetest kiss since their wedding day.

“Mmm. If I wasn’t incapacitated I’d show you what that kiss does to me. However, we have other things to discuss. Did you tell the sheriff?”

“I had one of the men ride to town and tell him. Everyone is going to be looking for William.”

“Then he’ll lie low. But he’s either in Golden City or Denver. He’ll stay close and he won’t be without his comforts. He’ll be somewhere with running water and a private bath.”

“Most of the hotels have running water but not all have private baths,” said

John. “I’ll tell the sheriff what you said. Checking the ones in Golden City won’t be a problem but in Denver, well that’s going to be harder. There are a lot of places to stay and not enough people to check them all.”

“Then we need to prepare ourselves. John, I need to learn to shoot.”

“No. I’ll have one of the men here with you and the girls all the time.”

“It’s not the same. I have to be alone sometimes. I have things to do and can’t expect the man to be with me all the time. The girls need to be able to play. I don’t want to take that away from them. You know this is the right thing. Just say I’m going to do it so I can kill snakes. Which will be true, no matter how you look at it. Whether a rattler or William, it’s still a snake.”

He took a deep breath and let it out in a long sigh. “Alright. I know when I’m out maneuvered. When your shoulder heals, I’ll start teaching you. But not a day before the doc says you’re good.”

“Deal.” She yawned though she tried not to. “I think I want to sleep now.”

“That’s good. The doc said you need to rest as much as possible.”

“Hmm hmm.” She moved so her head was pillowed on his chest rather than his arm. “Goodnight.”

She was fast asleep before he could return the phrase. He stayed there for a while, listening to her sleep. The soft, little snores that she would deny she made to her dying day.

He moved, replacing his chest with

her pillow and got up. Now that she was better he had work to do and a man to kill.

CHAPTER 9

It had been a couple of weeks since she'd been shot. And a week since she'd stop wearing the sling. She worked stretching her shoulder and getting it loose. She didn't want to lose the use of it so she moved it as much as possible. When no one was looking. Everyone seemed perfectly happy to keep her 'safe' and she was damn well tired of it.

She went into the kitchen after breakfast just as everyone was leaving.

"Everyone out. Now. That includes you John and you Bertha."

Bertha left. John stayed.

"Glad you're up and around," said John.

"I am too and I'm going to bake today. No. Don't even open your mouth to try and stop me."

He grinned at her. "Finally got bored did you?"

"I've been bored for two weeks. I just couldn't stand it any longer. I'm sorry if I hurt people's feelings but I've got to get busy."

He hooked his fingers in his belt loops and rocked back on his heels. "I figured you'd come around soon. It didn't hurt any that you kept the shoulder stationery while it healed but now you've got to move it to keep it working proper."

"Well it's working proper enough. Now leave if you want any pie at dinner or supper."

He came over and gave her a kiss on the cheek before he walked out the door. "Yes ma'am."

She wiped down the wooden counter. Then she got out the flour, salt and lard and went about making pie crusts for four pies. John had an apple tree in the yard and it was starting to produce more apples than they could use. Tomorrow, she thought, I'll get the kids and Bertha to help me gather apples and can them. For now she took an empty bushel basket and went out and picked a basket full of the sweet fruit.

Two hours later she had four apple pies cooling on the counter and it was time to start dinner. After that she'd make four more pies for supper. It was hard work and her arm ached from rolling out the dough but it was a good kind of ache. The ache you got from being useful.

Later that night when they laid in bed in the aftermath of their lovemaking, Sarah said, "You can't put me off any more. It's time to teach me how to shoot a gun."

"I know. As soon as I saw you working again in the kitchen, I knew I would have to do it. I still think it's unnecessary but I understand your need to be able to protect yourself. Admittedly I won't always be there."

"Yes." She leaned over and gave him a kiss on the cheek. "Thank you. When can we start?"

"Tomorrow after breakfast. Now

don't I get more than a peck on the cheek?"

"You already got your lovin' for tonight. Now lay back and go to sleep." She turned away from him, a smile on her face."

"Oh, no you don't. Just because we're not going to make love doesn't mean that you get to sleep yet. Come here." He pulled her into his embrace.

She giggled and cuddled into his side. If this wasn't love, she didn't know what love was. This comfort with each other, being able to talk together, make love to each other, not just have sex. This was love. It had to be. Now if she could just convince him of it.

The following day John took her out behind the barn. He'd set up some cans at varying distances to shoot at.

“I have a present for you.” He pulled the extra gun he carried from his belt. “I had the gun smith in Denver make this special for you. It’s a modified Colt revolver. It’s lighter and smaller than the Colt I carry. It shoots .22 ammunition rather than the .45 that mine does, but that’s plenty enough power to kill a man.”

She took the gun from his hand. It still seemed heavy to her. “Let me see your gun.” The difference was amazing. She had to use two a hands to hold his gun up. Hers she could do with one hand. She handed his gun back to him.

“Okay, I want you to hold the gun up and look down the barrel until you have the sight in line with the can on the far left. When you’ve got that where you want it, I want you to pull back the hammer and cock the gun, then I want you to just squeeze the trigger. Pull it gently and steadily, so the gun remains aimed where you want it to be. Too quick on the trigger and the gun will move and you'll miss your target."

She did as he asked and followed his instructions to the letter.

"Honey, that's real good, but you've got to keep your eyes open, too."

"I didn't realize I closed them."

He chuckled. "Just as soon as you started squeezing the trigger, you closed your eyes."

"Well that explains why I missed the can."

"That definitely could have something to do with it."

She practiced for most of the morning and eventually got to where she could hit the target two out of five times. More practice was needed but at least now she didn't feel totally defenseless. She put the gun in her apron pocket.

"Maybe we should get you a gun belt."

"It would look strange over my dress. The apron works fine and then I don't have little girls asking me what I'm doing with a gun."

"Good point."

"Thank you for teaching me. I feel a little safer."

"Just remember a gun is a last resort and it won't save you if the bad guy gets a hold of it. If you're going to use it, shoot to kill or don't carry it at all."

"I'll remember." And she would. There was no way William would get near her or her family again.

*****

William Grayson laid low in a Denver hotel. It wasn't the best but good enough to have the private bath he required. And better yet, they could be bribed to keep their mouths shut if the law came looking.

He hired more men to keep the ranch under watch. He knew Sarah hadn't died from the wound he inflicted on her. But it wasn't his fault. It was that husband of hers. If he'd just die, everything would be as it should be. Sarah would be his wife and they could put her brat in a boarding school somewhere out of the way.

He'd take it slow with Sarah once he had her. She was going to need some convincing that he was the best husband for her. He had to have her. Now that his mother was finally gone, he could. Mother always protected her from him. He tried convincing Sarah before she left but when she flat turned him down, he knew he'd have to let her go in order to keep track of her. He was afraid she'd run and he wouldn't know where to find her. She, unsuspecting as usual, gave him her new address. Told him to write. Ha! Write. And say what? I miss you and I'm going to have you one way or another?

They'd have to move to a new city. Couldn't take the chance of running into 'old' friends, though if truth be told, he didn't have friends. He had acquaintances and the only friend Sarah had was old lady Adams next door. It didn't matter now. He'd sold everything. They could live anywhere. Maybe they'd travel. Yes, they could go to Paris. It would be hard for Sarah to leave him in a city where she didn't speak the language and didn't have any money.

Wherever they went, he'd be glad to leave this place with its squeaky iron bed and worn carpets. There was barely room for his clothes in the old wardrobe and the commode was laughable. So small, the pitcher and basin almost didn't fit on top. A chamber pot would never have fit in the cupboard of the commode like it was supposed to. Good thing there was a toilet in the bathroom. Ah yes, the necessities to him were luxuries to these backward people.

Yes, he'd be very glad to get Sarah and leave the wretched West behind.

*****

Sarah began a new routine. Every

morning after breakfast she went out behind the barn to the target range John set up for her and practiced. Shooting again and again until she could hit the cans every four out of five times, consistently.

Sundays were different. After breakfast they headed to Golden City to church and when they got home she had to prepare dinner. No time for practice.

One Sunday, John invited their neighbor Nathan Ravenclaw for dinner. Nathan had lots of questions for Sarah. He wanted to know everything about Matchmaker & Company. She answered every one of them honestly. She told him Mrs. Selby checked out all her clients, both the bachelors and the brides. She had a knack for placing the right couples together.

"Nathan, are you thinking of getting a

mail order bride?" asked Sarah. She couldn't understand why he, or John for that matter, needed a mail order bride. Nathan was handsome in the extreme with black hair and eyes the color of a clear blue mountain lake as it reflects the sky on its still surface. They were mesmerizing. It seemed to her he would have his pick of women.

Of course, she thought the same thing about John, only to find out the marriageable women of his acquaintance were unwilling to take on the responsibility of a troubled child like Katy.

"I'm half Arapahoe Indian. No white woman will marry a half-breed and neither will an Arapahoe maiden. There are not a lot of options for someone like me. A mail order bride, especially one from back East won't have the same prejudices, if she accepts. She'll know what she's getting in to. It won't be easy but when I heard John had found the perfect bride, I got curious and asked John if I could talk to you."

"You flatter me. I'm not sure John would agree that I'm the perfect bride, but you can always talk to me. Any friend of Johns' is a friend to me."

"I don't flatter, Sarah. I only speak the truth. Thank you for a wonderful dinner, especially that pie. It was the best pie I've had in…well, I don't think I've ever had any that good."

She was inordinately pleased by his praise. "Hush now. You'll make me blush. You flatter me again, whether you mean to or not."

With dinner over Nathan said his

goodbyes, explaining he needed to get home and write Mrs. Selby. Sarah gave him her address.

"You can tell her we recommended her to you," said Sarah.

"Thanks. I will."

After he left Sarah told John, "The women out here are idiots. You and Nathan are prime husband material and any woman, including this woman, would be lucky to have you."

He grabbed her about her expanding waist and brought her close. He touched his lips to hers. "You say the nicest things." Deepening the kiss, his tongue mated with hers.

When he broke away they were both breathing hard. "I'd really like to take you upstairs right now."

"The girls are playing outside and Bertha is cleaning the kitchen. I'm free for the next hour. What about you?"

He leaned his forehead against hers. "I can't. We got in a couple of new horses that I need to work with. They're green broke but not fit for saddle horses yet."

"You're missing out."

"Don't I know it?" He gave her a quick kiss and left her standing there in the dining room…frustrated as hell.

She went to the shooting range to let off steam.

*****

William saw the two little girls playing outside. They were away from the house by a small stream. Easy pickings for someone as desperate as himself. This was his last chance and he knew it. He would either succeed or die. Sarah would come with him rather than have MaryAnn hurt. Having shot Sarah, even if by accident, would only further the belief that he could hurt MaryAnn, which, of course, he could. She was only a detriment to his ultimate goal of her mother.

He worked his way quietly upstream from the girls so the noise of the water would cover his coming. They were both too immersed in making mud pies and wading to notice his approach.

"Hello, MaryAnn."

Both girls turned toward him at the sound of his voice. They both screamed and started to run. William grabbed MaryAnn and let the other one go. But she turned and started kicking him. William took both girls by the hair and pulled until they stilled and he knew he was hurting them.

"Stop it both of you. Let me tell you what's going to happen. MaryAnn, you're going to come with me and you…what's your name?" He shook Katy by the hair.

"Katy," she said through her tears.

"Well Katy, you are going to tell Sarah to come to me alone right here, if she wants to see MaryAnn alive. Can you do that?"

When Katy didn't answer immediately he shook her. "Can you do that?" he repeated.

She nodded.

He shook her again.

"Yes, yes I can do that."

"Good. Off you go then, like a good little girl."

He let Katy go and she took off

running toward the house.

"Now, little MaryAnn. What shall we talk about? Hmm?"

"You're a bad man and my daddy is going to kill you."

"Your 'daddy' is dead and this new man will be too if he doesn't do exactly what I tell him to do."

"Mama will never go with you. She'll never leave us."

"That's precisely why she will come with me. She loves you. She won't want me to hurt you. And I will, you know." He shook her as if to prove his point. "I discovered long ago that I like hurting things. People are especially good. Although I haven't hurt a child in a long time, I doubt the pleasure is any less."

He smiled, could see the fear in her

eyes. She shut up.

Now he just had to wait. His plans and his dreams were coming true. In a few short hours Sarah would be his. He'd have to take the brat along to keep her mother in line, but he could do that. He knew now he wouldn't be able to send the kid away. If she was safe from him, Sarah would defy him but then again, watching her, seeing her fire tamed under his fist would be pleasurable too.

*****

Katy came running into the kitchen where she saw Bertha. "Where is Mama?"

"She's out on the shootin' range. What's the matter?"

Katy didn't answer but ran out of the house and down to the target range.

"Mama. Mama."

Sarah put her gun away in her apron. She hated for the girls to see her have it.

"Katy. Katy, what's the matter?"

"He's got her. The bad man has MaryAnn."

"What? Where?"

"Down by the crick where we play. He said to tell you he had her and to come alone if you wanted to see her alive."

Sarah squatted down so she was eye level with Katy. "I want you to go and find your daddy. Tell him everything you just told me and that I've gone to the creek to get MaryAnn."

Katy started crying again. "He said he'd hurt her and pulled our hair up until we stopped moving. I tried kicking him. I tried…" She took great gulps of air and cried all the harder.

Sarah took Katy in her arms. "It's all right. You did great, Katy. Now I'm going to go get MaryAnn back. You go find your daddy like I said, alright?"

She nodded and then threw her hands around Sarah. "Promise you won't go away. Promise you won't leave me."

"I promise. I'm not going anywhere, except to get MaryAnn. Okay?"

Katy sniffled and nodded.

"Now you go. Go get your daddy."

"Okay." She ran off in the direction of the corrals on the other side of the barn.

Sarah reloaded her gun as she walked. As soon as it was done, she took off at a run toward the stream. When she reached it what she saw made her blood run cold. William stood with his derringer pointed at MaryAnn who sat at the base of one of the old willow trees.

"Let her go, William. I came like you asked."

"Oh, I don't think so, dear cousin. The three of us are going to ride out of here and get on the first train going east. The sooner I get out of this backward country the better."

"How are we all going to ride out of here? Did you bring more than one horse?"

"No. I hadn't planned on taking the brat here, then I realized that you would be much more malleable if she was along. You see I don't have any qualms about hurting her if you don't do as I ask."

"You really shouldn't threaten my daughter, William. I don't like it." She moved her hand to her apron pocket. As soon as MaryAnn was safe she'd kill the bastard.

"Do you really think I care what you like? I let you go once. I thought that you'd come back when you discovered how primitive they are here, but you stayed. Why did you stay?"

"Why? Why else would I stay? I fell in love with my husband. I'll follow him anywhere and he's here, so am I. Do you really think I could ever love you? I cared for you once, as a brother, but no longer. The only thing I feel for you is pity, but I'll come with you. I'll go wherever you say, as soon as you let MaryAnn go."

He shook his head and pulled MaryAnn up. "The little one here is going to be in front of me and you're going to walk to my horse and get on it."

"Fine. Where is it?"

"Just upstream a short way."

Sarah walked up the stream, looking back over her shoulder at MaryAnn. "Don't worry, baby. It'll be alright. Just do as William says."

MaryAnn sniffled. Her tears dried up. "Yes, Mama."

"That's right. Everything is going to be right now. We'll be the family we always should have been." He laughed.

Chills snaked up Sarah's back. She realized William was totally insane, probably had been for some time, if not all his life. Why hadn't she seen it before?

Sarah got to the horse and waited for William to tell her what to do.

"Put MaryAnn on the horse."

Sarah did exactly what he said, helping MaryAnn into the saddle.

"Now, untie the horse and give the reins to the child."

Hope sprang in her chest. William didn't know MaryAnn could ride. She put the reins in her baby's hands.

"Lean down and ride for home, baby. Don't look back. Just go get Daddy." Sarah whispered.

"No talking, Sarah. Just do as I say."

Her mind worked frantically. She gave the reins to MaryAnn knowing what she was about to do was risky. Not to her daughter, MaryAnn could ride anything. She'd taken to riding like a fish to water. It was the timing. She put her hand in her apron pocket, turned and fired right through the cloth, hitting William in the knee.

The shot scared the horse as she knew it would and it would be a moment or two before MaryAnn got it under control, but Sarah didn't doubt she would.

William went down, fired his gun but the shot went wild. Sarah tried to get her gun out of her pocket but the barrel got caught in the hole.

"You shot me. You shot me." He leveled his gun at her. "That's the last time you'll shoot…."

A shot rang out. Sarah closed her eyes waiting for the pain. It didn't come. She looked at William. He lay dead in front of her.

Then she heard the thunder of hooves galloping toward her. John led the men, all armed. One of the wranglers brought up the rear, holding MaryAnn in front of him and leading her horse. He must have whisked her off the runaway gelding.

John jumped off his stallion before it even stopped. He ran to her and started running his hands over her.

"Are you hurt? Did he hit you?"

"No. I'm fine." She fell into his arms, tears streaming down her face. "You're here, I'm fine now."

"I haven't been so scared since you were wounded. I heard the shot, then saw him lying there with his gun trained on you. I prayed to God my aim was true."

"It was. I'm safe. MaryAnn is safe."

"Sarah, I love you. You, the girls and this new baby are my life. Without you I don't exist." He was crying.

She hugged him closer, her tears, tears of joy. "I love you, too. I'd never leave you voluntarily and now, with William dead, we're safe. Take me home, John.

Take me home."

Their tears mingled in their kiss. A kiss of promise and passion and all the good things to come.

He got into the saddle then pulled her up onto his lap.

"Joe, you and Sam take care of this riff raff. Bob, you ride for the sheriff. Tell him what happened and that he can come and get him."

Each man nodded and bent to the task.

Sarah leaned back into John, his chest cushioning her. He held her tight as though he was afraid he might lose her.

She turned her head and kissed his cheek. He turned his face until their lips met.

"When we get home I'm going to

show you how much I love you," he said.

"And I'm going to let you. But what about dinner and supper and your green broke horse?"

"Let them fend for themselves. Bertha can cook and feed the girls. I'm going to feast on you."

She giggled and he hugged her close.

When they got home, they told Bertha that she was cooking and said they would be indisposed.

"Where is Katy?" asked John.

"She's been scared to death. She's in her room with MaryAnn. That little one raced up there as soon as her feet hit the ground."

"We'll be back down to talk to you later," said John to Bertha.

She nodded. "I've got on the stew we

fixed this morning and there's plenty of bread and butter to go with it. No one is going to starve."

John and Sarah went up stairs to the girls' room. They found them wrapped in each other's arms both crying. When they saw their parents they broke apart and ran to their arms. John picked up both girls and carried them back to their bed. He sat and hugged his daughters, Sarah hugged them all.

They stayed that way for a while, all of them crying, thinking how close they came to losing one another. Fear abated as the reality that they were all safe sunk in.

"We're all fine. Your father and I love you very much and will always keep you safe."

They all held each other a while

longer until Sarah broke away. “You girls go down and tell Bertha I said you could have some milk and cookies. Tell her your daddy and I will be down later. Okay? Go on now.”

Sarah watched them run out of the room excited about getting a treat. She turned to John, “Let’s get reacquainted.”

John took her hand and led her across the hall to their room. He closed the door and slid the bolt home.

“I don’t want to be disturbed.”

Sarah let her apron fall, gun and all, to the floor, followed by her skirt, then she unbuttoned her blouse, taking her time with each button and never losing eye contact with her husband. When she was done she slid it off her shoulders to land in the growing pile at her feet.

John stepped toward her but she shook her head no and waggled her finger from side to side. He stopped.

Sarah sat on the bed and took off her boots then she pulled the bow at the top of the laces on her chemise and pulled it over her head. Then she stood and dropped her bloomers to the floor. She stepped out of the little pile of clothes and finally stood naked in front of her lover. Now she crooked her finger and let him come to her.

When he was arm's length away she stopped him. She stepped forward and unbuttoned his shirt, caressing his arms as she slipped it off his shoulders and onto the floor. Then she took his hand, led him to the bed and pushed him down onto it. She turned her back on him and raised his leg between hers and removed his boots. She wiggled her butt and looked coyly over her shoulder at him, watching his eyes darken before he stood.

"You tease me much more woman and I won't be responsible for my actions.

She laughed, the sound deep and throaty. Then she lay back on the bed and raised her arms to him. "No more teasing. Come to me, my love."

He came down over her bracing himself on his arms so he wouldn't crush her.

"I love you, Sarah, but I can't wait any longer." With those words he entered her in one swift stroke.

She welcomed him, as ready as he was. This time was slow, each of them conscious of the love they shared. Love that only moments ago they'd been afraid to mention. Fearful that it was not returned.

"When did you realize you loved me?" she asked.

"I knew when you were so sick after William shot you. But I think I fell for you when you blushed the very first time."

"You still make me blush. I think I fell for you the first night, too. When I saw you with Katy. How you didn't treat her any differently because she wouldn't speak. And then it was clenched the first time you held them both and let them cry all over you."

He moved within her.

"I'm so close. I'm going to come," she kept her eyes open and looked at the man she loved. He reached down between them and rubbed her pleasure bud until she shattered. Flew up out of her body and among the stars.

John followed, buried his face in her neck and collapsed on top of her.

She loved the feel of him on her. His big body covering hers, pushing her into the mattress. Of course, she could only take it for a short while before his size seemed to swamp her. He knew this and always rolled off of her before he became too much and she had to push him.

This time when he took her with him and clasped her to his side the feelings were different. She was different. The baby must have known it too; he kicked for the first time.

"Did you feel it? He kicked," said Sarah.

"I did." He took his hand and rubbed it over her belly, willing the baby to kick him again. He was rewarded for his efforts."

"I think he wants us to leave him alone," she laughed as John rubbed her stomach again, trying to get the baby's attention.

"Too bad. I want him to know his father."

"Oh, he will. He most certainly will."

They lay there, basking in their love for as long as they dared.

"We need to get up."

"I don't want to, "said Sarah.

"I didn't hurt you did I?" asked John, his hands roaming her body, checking for what he didn't know.

"No, you didn't hurt me. I loved it and I love you. I'd prefer to be able to spend the entire day in bed, but we can't. I shouldn't complain. Soon enough I won't be able to get out of bed and will be glad to be able to get up again."

"You didn't have any complications with MaryAnn did you?"

"No, everything went fine and it's all good with this one, too. You wait and see."

*****

Five Months Later

John paced the parlor. From the door across to the window in front of the sofa and behind the wing chairs. Back and forth again and again. His nerves were shot. He didn't remember being this nervous when Dorothy had Katy. Maybe because he didn't know any better or maybe because he didn't love Dorothy like he did Sarah. Nathan Ravenclaw came over to sit with him and he was thankful for the company even if he didn't talk to him much.

"Are you sure all this is worth it?" asked Nathan who was still a bachelor and had no children.

"She assures me it is. And I have to admit I don't know what I'd do without my girls. They and Sarah make me the man I am. Without them, I don't know what I'd be or where."

"I understand the need. I've decided to get a mail order bride. Mrs. Selby and I have corresponded and her man came to interview me last week. I gave you and Sarah as references. I hope that was alright."

John finally stopped his pacing and sat on the wing chair opposite Nathan.

"Of course. The man stopped by here

last week and talked to both Sarah and me. He made lots of notes and seemed pleased by what we said. I remember how nervous I was when he came to see me, but it all turned out good for me. The best thing I've ever done was get Sarah and MaryAnn. You'll be happy with the wife Mrs. Selby picks for you, as well. You may not think so to begin with, but she has a knack and it definitely worked for Sarah and me."

There was an anguished cry from upstairs. John popped up out of the chair and looked up toward the stairs.

"It was just Sarah. I know this is hard on you, but the Arapahoe women do this all the time. They put strips of rawhide between their teeth so they don't scream. Sarah would be a good Arapahoe."

Then they heard it. Sounds of boots

on the stairs. The doctor came into the parlor.

"Well, John you have a brand new son. Your wife would...."

John didn't hear what the doctor had to say after son. He bound up the stairs two at a time and ran down the hall to his and Sarah's bedroom. Bertha was helping Sarah into a fresh nightgown. The baby lay on the bed next to Sarah. John went to the bed just as Bertha finished. He sat on the edge of the bed next to her.

"You look beautiful."

"I look a mess. But I've done the most wonderful thing. Look at him. Isn't he beautiful?"

He looked at his son. So tiny and so perfect. Bertha hadn't swaddled him yet so John could count the fingers and toes. He saw his fine black hair and blue eyes. He was going to be a miniature of John and look more like MaryAnn than Katy.

"The girls are going to be excited when they get back from the Blacks. It was nice of Roger and Addie to offer to take the girls when the time came. I don't know what I would have done if they were here. I wasn't good company to Nathan."

Bertha came and swaddled the baby in a soft blanket then handed him to Sarah.

John lay back and put his arm around Sarah. She leaned back, cushioned by his chest and they admired their son.

"What shall we call him?" she asked.

"We could call him John Junior but I don't really like the idea of a junior. Maybe if my name were something other than John. What about your father, what was his name?"

"No, I won't name my son after the man who threw me out when I was pregnant with MaryAnn. What was your father's name?"

"Samuel."

"What about Samuel John Atwood. We'll call him Sam."

"I like that. Sam. Father would be proud."

They looked down at little Sam. He started to whimper and Sarah put him to her breast. With a little encouragement he began to nurse.

"He's beautiful." She brushed her hand over his downy head. "Just like his daddy."

"But he has his mother's eyes. He's going to look more like MaryAnn than anyone."

"That should please her. She and Katy are going to spoil him rotten. You know that don't you?"

"What else are big sister's for?"

He looked at his beautiful bride. "Thank you for giving me a son to go with our beautiful girls."

"Would you have been disappointed if he'd been a girl?"

"Never. You can't have too many girls."

"I intend to give you lots more of both."

"I intend to help you."

They laughed.

All the sons and daughters that followed were straight and tall. And loved by parents who were lucky enough to have found each other by mail.

ABOUT THE AUTHOR

Cynthia Woolf was born in Denver, Colorado and raised in the mountains west of Golden. She spent her early years running wild around the mountain side with her friends.

Their closest neighbor was one quarter of a mile away, so her little brother was her playmate and her best friend. That fierce friendship lasted until his death in 2006.

Cynthia was and is an avid reader. Her mother was a librarian and brought new books home each week. This is where young Cynthia first got the storytelling bug. She wrote her first story at the age of ten. A romance about a little boy she liked at the time.

She worked her way through college and went to work full time straight after graduation and there was little time to write. Then in 1990 she and two friends started a round robin writing a story about pirates. She found that she missed the writing and kept on with other stories. In 1992 she joined Colorado Romance Writers and Romance Writers of America. Unfortunately, the loss of her job demanded she not renew her memberships and her writing stagnated for many years.

In 2001, she saw an ad in the paper for a writers conference being put on by CRW and decided she'd attend. One of her favorite authors, Catherine Coulter, was the keynote speaker. Cynthia was lucky enough to have a seat at Ms. Coulter's table at the luncheon and after talking with her, decided she needed to get back to her writing. She rejoined both CRW and RWA that day and hasn't looked back.

Cynthia credits her wonderfully supportive husband Jim and the great friends she's made at CRW for saving her sanity and allowing her to explore her creativity.

ADDITIONAL TITLES AVAILABLE BY AUTHOR

CENTAURI DAWN

CENTAURI TWILIGHT

CENTAURI MIDNIGHT

TAME A WILD HEART

TAME A WILD WIND

TAME A WILD BRIDE

THE SWORDS OF GREGARA – JENALA

THE SWORDS OF GREGARA – RIZA

4591027R00172

Printed in Great Britain
by Amazon.co.uk, Ltd.,
Marston Gate.